Master Martin, the Cooper, and his Journeyman

By

E. T. A. Hoffmann

British Library Cataloguing-in-Publication Data
A catalogue record for this book is available from the
British Library

Contents

E. T. A. Hoffman

Ernst Theodor Wilhelm Hoffmann was born in Königsberg, East Prussia in 1776. His family were all jurists, and during his youth he was initially encouraged to pursue a career in law. However, in his late teens Hoffman became increasingly interested in literature and philosophy, and spent much of his time reading German classicists and attending lectures by, amongst others, Immanuel Kant.

In was in his twenties, upon moving with his uncle to Berlin, that Hoffman first began to promote himself as a composer, writing an operetta called Die Maske and entering a number of playwriting competitions. Hoffman struggled to establish himself anywhere for a while, flitting between a number of cities and dodging the attentions of Napoleon's occupying troops. In 1808, while living in Bamberg, he began his job as a theatre manager and a music critic, and Hoffman's break came a year later, with the publication of Ritter Gluck. The story centred on a man who meets, or thinks he has met, a long-dead composer, and played into the 'doppelgänger' theme – at that time very popular in literature. It was shortly after this that Hoffman began to use the pseudonym E. T. A. Hoffmann, declaring the 'A' to stand for 'Amadeus', as a tribute to the great composer, Mozart.

Over the next decade, while moving between Dresden, Leipzig and Berlin, Hoffman produced a great range of both literary and musical works. Probably Hoffman's most well-known story, produced in 1816, is 'The Nutcracker and the Mouse King', due to the fact that – some seventy-six years later - it inspired Tchaikovsky's ballet The Nutcracker.

In the same vein, his story 'The Sandman' provided both the inspiration for Léo Delibes's ballet Coppélia, and the basis for a highly influential essay by Sigmund Freud, called 'The Uncanny'. (Indeed, Freud referred to Hoffman as the "unrivalled master of the uncanny in literature.")

Alcohol abuse and syphilis eventually took a great toll on Hoffman though, and – having spent the last year of his life paralysed – he died in Berlin in 1822, aged just 46. His legacy is a powerful one, however: He is seen as a pioneer of both Romanticism and fantasy literature, and his novella, Mademoiselle de Scudéri: A Tale from the Times of Louis XIV is often cited as the first ever detective story.

How Master Martin was elected "Candle-master" and how he returned thanks therefor.

On the 1st of May, 1580, in accordance with traditionary custom and usage, the honourable guild of coopers, or wine-cask makers, of the free Imperial Town of Nuremberg, held with all due ceremony a meeting of their craft. A short time previously one of the presidents, or "Candle-masters," as they were called, had been carried to his grave; it was therefore necessary to elect a successor. Choice fell upon Master Martin. And in truth there was scarcely another who could be measured against him in the building of strong and well-made casks; none understood so well as he the management of wine in the cellar;1 hence he counted amongst his customers very many men of distinction, and lived in the most prosperous circumstances — nay, almost rolled in riches. Accordingly, after Martin had been elected, the worthy Councillor Jacobus Paumgartner, who, in his official character of syndic,2 presided over the meeting, said, "You have done bravely well, friends, to choose Master Martin as your president, for the office could not be in better hands. He is held in high esteem by all who know him, not only on account of his great skill, but on account of his ripe experience in the art of keeping and managing the rich juice of the grape. His steady industry and upright life, in spite of all the wealth he has amassed, may serve as an example to you all. Welcome then a thousand times, goodman Master Martin, as our honoured president."

With these words Paumgartner rose to his feet and took a few steps forward, with open arms, expecting that Martin would come to meet him. The latter immediately placed both his hands upon the arms of his chair and raised himself as expeditiously as his portly person would permit him to rise,— which was only slowly and heavily. Then just as slowly he strode into Paumgartner's hearty embrace, which, however, he scarcely returned. "Well," said Paumgartner, somewhat nettled at this, "well, Master Martin, are you not altogether well pleased that we have elected you to be our 'Candle-master'?" Master Martin, as was his wont, threw his head back into his neck, played with his fingers upon his capacious belly, and, opening his eyes wide and thrusting forward his under-lip with an air of superior astuteness, let his eyes sweep round the assembly. Then, turning to Paumgartner, he began, "Marry, my good and worthy sir, why should I not be altogether well pleased, seeing that I receive what is my due? Who refuses to take the reward of his honest labour? Who turns away from his threshold the defaulting debtor when at length he comes to pay his long standing debt? What! my good sirs," and Martin turned to the masters who sat around, "what! my good sirs, has it then occurred to you at last that I— I must be president of our honourable guild? What do you look for in your president? That he be the most skilful in workmanship? Go look at my two-tun cask made without fire,3 my brave masterpiece, and then come and tell me if there's one amongst you dare boast that, so far as concerns thoroughness and finish, he has ever turned out anything like it. Do you desire that your president possess money and goods? Come to my house and I will throw open chests and drawers, and you shall feast your eyes on the glitter of the sparkling gold and silver. Will you have a president who is respected by noble and base-born alike? Only ask our honoured gentlemen of the Council, ask the princes and noblemen around our good town of Nuremberg, ask his Lordship, the Bishop of Bamberg, ask what they all think of Master Martin? Oh! I— I don't think you'll hear much said against him." At the same time Master Martin struck his big fat belly with the greatest self-satisfaction, smiling with his eyes half-closed. Then, as all remained silent, nothing being heard except a dubious clearing of the throat here and there, he continued, "Ay! ay! I see. I ought, I know very well, to thank you all handsomely that in this election the good Lord above has at last seen fit to enlighten your minds. Well, when I receive the price of my labour, when my debtor repays me the borrowed money, I write at the bottom of the bill or of the receipt my 'Paid with thanks, Thomas4 Martin, Master-cooper here.' Let me then thank you all from my heart, since in electing me to be your president and 'Candle-master' you have wiped out an old debt. As for the rest, I pledge you that I will discharge the duties of my office with all fidelity and uprightness. In the hour of need I will stand by the guild and by each of you to the very best of my abilities with word and deed. I will exert the utmost diligence to uphold the honour and fame of our celebrated handicraft, without bating one jot of its present credit. My honoured syndic, and all you, my good friends and masters, I invite to come and partake of good cheer with me on the coming Sunday. Then, with blithesome hearts and minds, let us deliberate over a glass of good Hochheimer5 or Johannisberger,6 or any other choice wine in my cellar that your palates may crave, what can be done for the furtherance of our common weal. Once again, I say you shall be all heartily welcome."

The honest masters' countenances, which had perceptibly clouded on hearing Master Martin's proud words, now recovered their serenity, whilst the previous dead silence was followed by the cheerful buzz of conversation, in which a good deal was said about Master Martin's great deserts, and also about his choice cellar. All promised to be present on the Sunday, and offered their hands to the newly-elected "Candle-master," who took them and shook them warmly, also drawing a few of the masters a little towards him, as if desirous of embracing them. The company separated in blithe good-humour.

1 Wine was frequently stored at this period on the cooper's premises in huge casks, and afterwards drawn off in smaller casks and bottled.

2 In many Mediæval German towns the rulers (Burgomaster and Councillors) were mostly self-elected, power being in the hands of a few patrician families. A Councillor generally attended a full meeting of a guild as a sort of "patron" or "visitor." Compare the position which Sir Patrick Charteris occupied with respect to the good citizens of Perth. (See Sir Walter Scott's Fair Maid of

Perth , chap. vii., et passim .)

3 *The well-known Great Cask of Heidelberg, built for the Elector Palatine Ernest Theodore in 1751, is calculated to hold 49,000 gallons, and is 32 feet long and 26 feet in diameter. This is not the only gigantic wine cask that has been made in Germany. Other monsters are now in the cellars at Tübingen (made in 1546), Groningen (1678), Königstein (1725), &c.*

4 *Hoffmann calls him Tobias also lower down, and then Thomas again.*

5 *Hochheimer is the name of a Rhine wine that has been celebrated since the beginning of the ninth century, and is grown in the neighbourhood of Hochheim, a town in the district of Wiesbaden.*

6 *Johannisberger is also grown near Wiesbaden. The celebrated vineyard is said to cover only 39–1/2 acres.*

What afterwards took place in Master Martin's house.

Now it happened that Councillor Jacobus Paumgartner had to pass by Master Martin's in order to reach his own home; and as they both stood outside Master Martin's door, and Paumgartner was about to proceed on his way, his friend, doffing his low bonnet, and bowing respectfully and as low as he was able, said to him, "I should be very glad, my good and worthy sir, if you would not disdain to step in and spend an hour or so in my humble house. Be pleased to suffer me to derive both profit and entertainment from your wise conversation." "Ay, ay! Master Martin, my friend," replied Paumgartner smiling, "gladly enough will I stay a while with you; but why do you call your house a humble house? I know very well that there's none of the richest of our citizens who can excel you in jewels and valuable furniture. Did you not a short time ago complete a handsome building which makes your house one of the ornaments of our renowned Imperial Town?1 In respect of its interior fittings I say nothing, for no patrician even need be ashamed of it."

Old Paumgartner was right; for on opening the door, which was brightly polished and richly ornamented with brass-work, they stepped into a spacious entrance hall almost resembling a state-room; the floor was tastefully inlaid, fine pictures hung on the walls, and the cupboards and chairs were all artistically carved. And all who came in willingly obeyed the direction inscribed in verses, according to olden custom, on a tablet which hung near the door:—

12

Let him who will the stairs ascend
See that his shoes be rubbed well clean.
Or taken off were better, I ween;
He thus avoids what might offend.
A thoughtful man is well aware
How he indoors himself should bear.

It had been a hot day, and now as the hour of twilight was approached it began to be close and stuffy in the rooms, so Master Martin led his eminent guest into the cool and spacious parlour-kitchen. For this was the name applied at that time to a place in the houses of the rich citizens which, although furnished as a kitchen, was never used as such — all kinds of valuable utensils and other necessaries of housekeeping being there set out on show. Hardly had they got inside the door when Master Martin shouted in a loud voice, "Rose, Rose!" Then the door was immediately opened, and Rose, Master Martin's only daughter, came in.

I should like you, dear reader, to awaken at this moment a vivid recollection of our great Albrecht Dürer's masterpieces; I would wish that the glorious maidens whom we find in them, with all their noble grace, their sweet gentleness and piety, should recur to your mind, endowed with living form. Recall the noble and delicate figure, the beautifully arched, lily-white forehead, the carnation flitting like a breath of roses across the cheek, the full sweet cherry-red lips,— recall the eyes full of pious aspirations, half-veiled by their dark lashes, like moonlight seen through dusky foliage,— recall the silky hair, artfully gathered into graceful plaits,— recall the divine beauty of these maidens, and you will see lovely Rose. How else than in this way could the narrator sketch the dear, darling child? And yet permit me to remind you here of an admirable young artist into whose heart a quickening ray has fallen from these beautiful old times. I mean the German painter Cornelius,2 in Rome. Just as Margaret looks in Cornelius's drawings to Goethe's mighty Faust when she utters the words, "Bin weder Fräulein noch schön"3 (I am neither a lady of rank, nor yet beautiful), so also may Rose have looked when in the shyness of her pure chaste heart she felt compelled to shun addresses that smacked somewhat too much of freedom.

Rose bowed low with child-like respect before Paumgartner, and taking his hand, pressed it to her lips. The crimson colour rushed into the old gentleman's pale cheeks, as the sun when setting shoots up a dying flash, suddenly converting the dark foliage into gold, so the fire of a youth now left far behind gleamed once more in his eyes. "Ay! ay!" he cried in a blithesome voice, "marry, my good friend Master Martin, you are a rich and a prosperous man, but the best of all the blessings which the good Lord has given you is your lovely daughter Rose. If the hearts of old gentlemen like us who sit in the Town Council are so stirred that we cannot turn away our purblind eyes from the dear child, who can find fault with the young folks if they stop and stand like blocks of wood, or as if spell-bound, when they meet your daughter in the street, or see her at church, though we have a word of blame for our clerical gentry, because on the

Allerwiese,4 or wherever else a festival is held, they all crowd round your daughter, with their sighs, and loving glances, and honied words, to the vexation of all other girls? Well, well, Master Martin, you can choose you your son-inlaw amongst any of our young patricians, or wherever else you may list."

A dark frown settled on Master Martin's face; he bade his daughter fetch some good old wine; and after she had left the room, the hot blushes mantling thick and fast upon her cheeks, and her eyes bent upon the floor, he turned to old Paumgartner, "Of a verity, my good sir, Heaven has dowered my daughter with exceptional beauty, and herein too I have been made rich; but how can you speak of it in the girl's presence? And as for a patrician son-inlaw, there'll never be anything of that sort." "Enough, Master Martin, say no more," replied Paumgartner, laughing. "Out of the fulness of the heart the mouth must speak. Don't you believe, then, that when I set eyes on Rose the sluggish blood begins to leap in my old heart also? And if I do honestly speak out what she herself must very well know, surely there's no very great mischief done."

Rose brought the wine and two beautiful drinking-glasses. Then Martin pushed the heavy table, which was ornamented with some remarkable carving, into the middle of the kitchen. Scarcely, however, had the old gentlemen taken their places and Master Martin had filled the glasses when a trampling of horses was heard in front of the house. It seemed as if a horseman had pulled up, and as if his voice was heard in the entrance-passage below. Rose hastened down

15

and soon came back with the intelligence that old Junker5 Heinrich von Spangenberg was there and wished to speak to Master Martin. "Marry!" cried Martin, "now this is what I call a fine lucky evening, which brings me my best and oldest customer. New orders of course, I see I shall have to 'cask' out again"— Therewith he hastened down as fast as he was able to meet his welcome guest.

1 Nuremberg is noted for its interesting old houses with high narrow gables turned next the street: amongst the most famous are those belonging to the families of Nassau, Tucher, Peller, Petersen (formerly Toppler), and those of Albrecht Dürer and of Hans Sachs, the cobbler-poet of the 16th century.

2 Peter von Cornelius (1783–1867), founder of a great German school of historical painting. Going to Rome in 1811, he painted a set of seven scenes illustrative of Goethe's Faust, having previously finished a set at Frankfort (on Main). Amongst his many famous works are the Last Judgment in the Ludwig Church at Munich and frescoes in the Glyptothek there.

3 Gretchen's real words were "Bin weder Fräulein weder schön." See the scene which follows the "Hexenküche" scene in the first part of Faust.

4 A meadow or common on the outskirts of the town, which served as a general place of recreation and amusement. Nearly every German town has such; as the Theresa Meadow at Munich, the Canstatt Meadow near Stuttgart, the Communal Meadow on the right bank of the Main not far from Frankfort (see Goethe, Wahrheit und Dichtung, near the beginning), &c.

5 *This word is generally used to designate an untitled country nobleman, a member of an old-established noble "county" family. In Prussia the name came to be applied to a political party. A most interesting description of the old Prussian Junker is given in Wilibald Alexis' (W. H. Häring's) charming novel Die Hosen des Herrn v. Bredow (1846–48), in Sir Walter Scott's style.*

How Master Martin extols his trade above all others.

The Hochheimer sparkled in the beautiful cut drinking-glasses, and loosened the tongues and opened the hearts of the three old gentlemen. Old Spangenberg especially, who, though advanced in years, was yet brimming with freshness and vivacity, had many a jolly prank out of his merry youth to relate, so that Master Martin's belly wabbled famously, and again and again he had to brush the tears out of his eyes, caused by his loud and hearty laughing. Herr Paumgartner, too, forgot more than was customary with him the dignity of the Councillor, and enjoyed right well the noble liquor and the merry conversation. But when Rose again made her appearance with the neat housekeeper's basket under her arm, out of which she took a tablecloth as dazzling white as fresh-fallen snow,— when she tripped backwards and forwards busy with household matters, laying the cloth, and placing a plentiful supply of appetising dishes on the table,— when, with a winning smile she invited the gentlemen not to despise what had been hurriedly prepared, but to turn to and eat — during all this time their conversation and laughter ceased. Neither Paumgartner nor Spangenberg averted their sparkling eyes from the fascinating maiden, whilst Master Martin too, leaning back in his chair, and folding his hands, watched her busy movements with a gratified smile. Rose was withdrawing, but old Spangenberg was on his feet in a moment, quick as a youth; he took the girl by both shoulders and cried, again and again, as the bright tears trickled from his eyes, "Oh you good, you sweet little angel! What a dear darling girl you are!" then he kissed her twice — three times on the forehead, and returned to his seat, apparently in deep thought.

Paumgartner proposed the toast of Rose's health. "Yes," began Spangenberg, after she had gone out of the room, "yes, Master Martin, Providence has given you a precious jewel in your daughter, whom you cannot well over-estimate. She will yet bring you to great honour. Who is there, let him be of what rank in life he may, who would not willingly be your son-inlaw?" "There you are," interposed Paumgartner; "there you see, Master Martin, the noble Herr von Spangenberg is exactly of my opinion. I already see our dear Rose a patrician's bride with the rich jewellery of pearls1 in her beautiful flaxen hair." "My dear sirs," began Martin, quite testily, "why do you, my dear sirs, keep harping upon this matter — a matter to which I have not as yet directed my thoughts? My Rose has only just reached her eighteenth year; it's not time for such a young thing to be looking out for a lover. How things may turn out afterwards — well, that I leave entirely to the will of the Lord; but this I do at any rate know, that none shall touch my daughter's hand, be he patrician or who he may, except the cooper who approves himself the cleverest and skilfullest master in his trade — presuming, of course, that my daughter will have him, for never will I constrain my dear child to do anything in the world, least of all to make a marriage that she does not like." Spangenberg and Paumgartner looked at each other, perfectly astonished at this extraordinary decision of the Master's.2 At length, after some clearing of his throat, Spangenberg began, "So, then, your daughter is not to wed out of her own station?" "God forbid she should," rejoined Martin. "But," continued Spangenberg, "if now a skilled master of a higher trade, say a goldsmith, or even a brave young artist, were to sue for your Rose and succeeded in winning her favour more than all other young journeymen, what then?" "I should say," replied Master Martin, throwing his head back into his neck, "show me, my excellent young friend, the fine two-tun cask which you have made as your masterpiece; and if he could not do so, I should kindly open the door for him and very politely request him to try his luck elsewhere." "Ah! but," went on Spangenberg again, "if the young journeyman should reply, 'A little structure of that kind I cannot show you, but come with me to the market-place and look at yon beautiful house which is sending up its slender gable into the free open air — that's my masterpiece.'" "Ah! my good sir, my good sir," broke in Master Martin impatiently, "why do you give yourself all this trouble to try and make me alter my conviction? Once and for all, my son-inlaw must be of my trade; for my trade I hold to be the finest trade there is in the world. Do you think we've nothing to do but to fix the staves into the trestles (hoops), so that the cask may hold together? Marry, it's a fine thing and an admirable thing that our handiwork requires a previous knowledge of the way in which that noble blessing of Heaven, good wine, must be kept and managed, that it may acquire strength and flavour so as to go through all our veins and warm our blood like the true spirit of life! And then as for the construction of the casks — if we are to turn out a successful piece of work, must we not first draw out our plans with compass and rule? We must be arithmeticians and geometricians of no mean attainments, how else can we adapt the proportion and size of the cask to the measure of its contents? Ay, sir, my heart laughs in my body when we've bravely laboured at the staves with jointer and adze and have gotten a brave cask in the vice; and then when my journeymen swing their mallets and down it comes on the drivers clipp! clapp! clipp! clapp!— that's merry music for you; and there stands your well-made cask. And of a verity I may look a little proudly about me when I take my marking-tool in my hand and mark the sign of my handiwork, that is known and honoured of all respectable wine-masters, on the bottom of the cask. You spoke of house-building, my good sir. Well, a beautiful house is in truth a glorious piece of work, but if I were a house-builder and went past a house I had built, and saw a dirty fellow or good-for-nothing rascal who had got possession of it looking down upon me from the bay-window, I should feel thoroughly ashamed,— I should feel, purely out of vexation and annoyance, as if I should like to pull down and destroy my own work. But nothing like that can happen with the structures I build. Within them there comes and lives once for all nothing but the purest spirit on earth — good wine. God prosper my handiwork!"

"That's a fine eulogy," said Spangenberg, "and honestly and well meant. It does you honour to think so highly of your craft; but — do not get impatient if I keep harping upon the same string — now if a patrician really came and sued for your daughter? When a thing is brought right home to a man it often looks very different from what he thought it would." "Why, i' faith," cried Master Martin somewhat vehemently, "why, what else could I do but make a polite bow and say, 'My dear sir, if you were a brave cooper, but as it is'"—— "Stop a bit," broke in Spangenberg again; "but if now some fine day a handsome Junker on a gallant horse, with a brilliant retinue dressed in magnificent silks and satins, were to pull up before your door and ask you for Rose to wife?" "Marry, by my faith," cried Master Martin still more vehemently than before, "why, marry, I should run down as fast as I could and lock and bolt the door, and I should shout 'Ride on farther! Ride on farther! my worshipful Herr Junker; roses like mine don't blossom for you. My wine-cellar and my money-bags would, I dare say, suit you passing well — and you would take the girl in with the bargain; but ride on! ride on farther.'" Old Spangenberg rose to his feet, his face hot and red all over; then, leaning both hands on the table, he stood looking on the floor before him. "Well," he began after a pause, "and now the last question, Master Martin. If the Junker before your door were my own son, if I myself stopped at your door, would you shut it then, should you believe then that we were only come for your wine-cellar and your money-bags?" "Not at all, not at all, my good and honoured sir," replied Master Martin. "I would gladly throw open my door, and everything in my house should be at your and your son's service; but as for my Rose, I should say to you, 'If it had only pleased Providence to make your gallant son a brave cooper, there would be no more welcome son-inlaw on earth than he; but now'—— But, my dear good sir, why do you tease and worry me with such curious questions? See you, our merry talk has come abruptly to an end, and look! our glasses are all standing full. Let's put all sons-inlaw and Rose's marriage aside; here, I pledge you to the health of your son, who is, I hear, a handsome young knight." Master Martin seized his glass; Paumgartner followed his example, saying, "A truce to all captious conversation, and here's a health to your gallant son." Spangenberg touched glasses with them, and said with a forced smile, "Of course you know I was only speaking in jest; for nothing but wild head-strong passion could ever lead my son, who may choose him a wife from amongst the noblest families in the land, so far to disregard his rank and birth as to sue for your daughter. But methinks you might have answered me in a somewhat more friendly way." "Well, but, my good sir," replied Master Martin, "even in jest I could only speak as I should act if the wonderful things you are pleased to imagine were really to happen. But you must let me have my pride; for you cannot but allow that I am the skilfullest cooper far and near, that I understand the management of wine, that I observe strictly and truly the admirable wine-regulations of our departed Emperor Maximilian3 (may he rest in peace!), that as beseems a pious man I abhor all godlessness, that I never burn more than one small half-ounce of pure sulphur4 in one of my two-tun

23

casks, which is necessary to preserve it — the which, my good and honoured sirs, you will have abundantly remarked from the flavour of my wine." Spangenberg resumed his seat, and tried to put on a cheerful countenance, whilst Paumgartner introduced other topics of conversation. But, as it so often happens, when once the strings of an instrument have got out of tune, they are always getting more or less warped, so that the player in vain tries to entice from them again the full-toned chords which they gave at first, thus it was with the three old gentlemen; no remark, no word, found a sympathetic response. Spangenberg called for his grooms, and left Master Martin's house quite in an ill-humour after he had entered it in gay good spirits.

1 A string of pearls worn on the wedding-day was a prerogative of a patrician bride.

2 In the Middle Ages, in Nuremberg, and in most other industrial towns also, the artisans and others who formed guilds (each respective trade or calling having generally its guild) were divided into three grades, masters, journeymen, and apprentices. Admission from one of these grades into the one next above it was subject to various more or less restrictive conditions. A man could only become a "master" and regularly set up in business for himself after having gone through the various stages of training in conformity with the rules or prescriptions of his guild, after having constructed his masterpiece to the satisfaction of a specially appointed commission, and after fulfilling certain requirements as to age, citizenship, and in some cases possession of a certain amount of property. It was usual for journeymen to spend a certain time in travelling going from one centre of their trade to another.

3 From another passage (Der Feind, chap. i) it appears that the reference is to a series of regulations dealing with the wine industry, of date August 24, 1498, in the reign of Maximilian I.

4 Sulphur is burnt inside the cask (care being taken that it does not touch it) in order to keep it sweet and pure, as well as to impart both flavour and colour to the wine.

The old Grandmother's Prophecy.

Master Martin was rather ill at ease because his brave old customer had gone away out of humour in this way, and he said to Paumgartner, who had just emptied his last glass and rose to go too, "For the life of me, I can't understand what the old gentleman meant by his talk, and why he should have got testy about it at last." "My good friend Master Martin," began Paumgartner, "you are a good and honest man; and a man has verily a right to set store by the handiwork he loves and which brings him wealth and honour; but he ought not to show it in boastful pride, that's against all right Christian feeling. And in our guild-meeting today you did not act altogether right in putting yourself before all the other masters. It may true that you understand more about your craft than all the rest; but that you go and cast it in their teeth can only provoke ill-humour and black looks. And then you must go and do it again this evening! You could not surely be so infatuated as to look for anything else in Spangenberg's talk beyond a jesting attempt to see to what lengths you would go in your obstinate pride. No wonder the worthy gentleman felt greatly annoyed when you told him you should only see common covetousness in any Junker's wooing of your daughter. But all would have been well if, when Spangenberg began to speak of his son, you had interposed — if you had said, 'Marry, my good and honoured sir, if you yourself came along with your son to sue for my daughter — why, i' faith, that would be far too high

26

an honour for me, and I should then have wavered in my firmest principles.' Now, if you had spoken to him like that, what else could old Spangenberg have done but forget his former resentment, and smile cheerfully and in good humour as he had done before?" "Ay, scold me," said Master Martin, "scold me right well, I have well deserved it; but when the old gentleman would keep talking such stupid nonsense I felt as if I were choking, I could not make any other answer." "And then," went on Paumgartner, "what a ridiculous resolve to give your daughter to nobody but a cooper! You will commit, you say, your daughter's destiny to Providence, and yet with human shortsightedness you anticipate the decree of the Almighty in that you obstinately determine beforehand that your son-inlaw is to come from within a certain narrow circle. That will prove the ruin of you and your Rose, if you are not careful Have done, Master Martin, have done with such unchristian childish folly; leave the Almighty, who will put a right choice in your daughter's honest heart when the right time comes — leave Him to manage it all in his own way." "O my worthy friend," said Master Martin, quite crest-fallen, "I now see how wrong I was not to tell you everything at first. You think it is nothing but overrating my handiwork that has brought me to take this unchangeable resolve of wedding Rose to none but a master-cooper; but that is not so; there is another reason, a more wonderful and mysterious reason. I can't let you go until you have learned all; you shall not bear ill-will against me over-night. Sit down, I earnestly beg you, stay a few minutes longer. See here; there's still a bottle of that old wine left which the ill-tempered Junker has despised; come, let's enjoy it together." Paumgartner was astonished at Master Martin's earnest, confidential tone, which was in general perfectly foreign to his nature; it seemed as if there was something weighing heavy upon the man's heart that he wanted to get rid of.

And when Paumgartner had taken his seat and drunk a glass of wine, Master Martin began as follows. "You know, my good and honoured friend, that soon after Rose was born I lost my beloved wife; Rose's birth was her death. At that time my old grandmother was still living, if you can call it living when one is blind, deaf as a post, scarce able to speak, lame in every limb, and lying in bed day after day and night after night Rose had been christened; and the nurse sat with the child in the room where my old grandmother lay. I was so cut up with grief, and when I looked upon my child, so sad and yet so glad — in fact I was so greatly shaken that I felt utterly unfitted for any kind of work, and stood quite still and wrapped up in my own thoughts beside my old grandmother's bed; and I counted her happy, since now all her earthly pain was over. And as I gazed upon her face a strange smile began to steal across it, her withered features seemed to be smoothed out, her pale cheeks became flushed with colour. She raised herself up in bed; she stretched out her paralysed arms, as if suddenly animated by some supernatural power,— for she had never been able to do so at other times. She called distinctly in a low pleasant voice, 'Rose, my darling Rose!' The nurse got up and brought her the child, which she rocked up and down in her arms. But then, my good sir, picture my utter astonishment, nay, my alarm, when the old lady struck up in a clear strong voice a song in the Hohe fröhliche Lobweis 1 of Herr Hans Berchler, mine host of the Holy Ghost in Strasburg, which ran like this —

Maiden tender, with cheeks so red,
Rose, listen to the words I say;
Wouldst guard thyself from fear and ill?
Then put thy trust in God alway;
Let not thy tongue at aught make mock,
Nor foolish longings feed at heart.
A vessel fair to see he'll bring,
In which the spicy liquid foams,
And bright, bright angels gaily sing.
And then in reverent mood
Hearken to the truest love,
Oh! hearken to the sweet love-words.
The vessel fair with golden grace —
Lo! him who brings it in the house
Thou wilt reward with sweet embrace;
And an thy lover be but true,
Thou need'st nor wait thy father's kiss.
The vessel fair will always bring
All wealth and joy and peace and bliss;
So, virgin fair, with the bright, bright eyes,
Let aye thy little ear be ope
To all true words. And henceforth live,

And with God's richest blessing thrive.

"And after she had sung this song through, she laid the child gently and carefully down upon the coverlet; and, placing her trembling withered hand upon her forehead, she muttered something to herself, to us, however, unintelligible; but the rapt countenance of the old lady showed in every feature that she was praying. Then her head sank back upon the pillows, and just as the nurse took up the child my old grandmother took a deep breath; she was dead." "That is a wonderful story," said Paumgartner when Master Martin ceased speaking; "but I don't exactly see what is the connection between your old grandmother's prophetic song and your obstinate resolve to give Rose to none but a master-cooper." "What!" replied Master Martin, "why, what can be plainer than that the old lady, especially inspired by the Lord at the last moments of her life, announced in a prophetic voice what must happen if Rose is to be happy? The lover who is to bring wealth and joy and peace and bliss into the house with his vessel fair, who is that but a lusty cooper who has made his vessel fair, his masterpiece with me? In what other vessel does the spicy liquid foam, if not in the wine-cask? And when the wine works, it bubbles and even murmurs and splashes; that's the lovely angels chasing each other backwards and forwards in the wine and singing their gay songs. Ay, ay, I tell you, my old grandmother meant none other lover than a master-cooper; and it shall be so, it shall be so." "But, my good Master Martin," said Paumgartner, "you are interpreting the words of your old grandmother just in your own way. Your interpretation is far from satisfactory to my mind; and I repeat that you ought to leave all simply to the ordering of Providence and your daughter's heart, in which I dare be bound the right choice lies hidden away somewhere." "And I repeat," interrupted Martin impatiently, "that my son-inlaw shall be,— I am resolved,— shall be none other than a skilful cooper." Paumgartner almost got angry at Master Martin's stubbornness; he controlled himself, however, and, rising from his seat, said, "It's getting late, Master Martin, let us now have done with our drinking and talking, for neither methinks will do us any more good."

When they came out into the entrance-hall, there stood a young woman with five little boys, the eldest scarce eight years old apparently, and the youngest scarce six months. She was weeping and sobbing bitterly. Rose hastened to meet the two old gentlemen and said, "Oh father, father! Valentine is dead; there is his wife and the children." "What! Valentine dead?" cried Master Martin, greatly startled. "Oh! that accident! that accident! Just fancy," he continued, turning to Paumgartner, "just fancy, my good sir, Valentine was the cleverest journeyman I had on the premises; and he was industrious, and a good honest man as well. Some time ago he wounded himself dangerously with the adze in building a large cask; the wound got worse and worse; he was seized with a violent fever, and now he has had to die of it in the prime of life." Thereupon Master Martin approached the poor disconsolate woman, who, bathed in tears, was lamenting

31

that she had nothing but misery and starvation staring her in the face. "What!" said Master Martin, "what do you think of me then? Your husband got his dangerous wound whilst working for me, and do you think I am going to let you perish of want? No, you all belong to my house from now onwards. To-morrow, or whenever you like, we'll bury your poor husband, and then do you and your boys go to my farm outside the Ladies Gate,2 where my fine open workshop is, and where I work every day with my journeymen. You can install yourself as housekeeper there to look after things for me, and your fine boys I will educate as if they were my own sons. And, I tell you what, I'll take your old father as well into my house. He was a sturdy journeyman cooper once upon a time whilst he still had muscle in his arms. And now — if he can no longer wield the mallet, or the beetle or the beak iron, or work at the bench, he yet can do something with croze-adze, or can hollow out staves for me with the draw-knife. At any rate he shall come along with you and be taken into my house." If Master Martin had not caught hold of the woman, she would have fallen on the floor at his feet in a dead swoon, she was so affected by grief and emotion. The eldest of the boys clung to his doublet, whilst the two youngest, whom Rose had taken in her arms, stretched out their tiny hands towards him, as if they had understood it all. Old Paumgartner said, smiling and with bright tears standing in his eyes, "Master Martin, one can't bear you any ill-will;" and he betook himself to his own home.

1 See note 2, p. 15. The German Meistersinger always sang without any accompaniment of musical instruments.

2 This is one of the principal round towers, erected 1558–1568, in the town walls; it is situated on the south-east.

How the two young journeymen Frederick and Reinhold became acquainted with each other.

Upon a beautiful, grassy, gently-sloping hill, shaded by lofty trees, lay a fine well-made young journeyman, whose name was Frederick. The sun had already set, and rosy tongues of light were stretching upwards from the furthest verge of the horizon. In the distance the famed imperial town of Nuremberg could be plainly seen, spreading across the valley and boldly lifting up her proud towers against the red glow of the evening, its golden rays gilding their pinnacles. The young journeyman was leaning his arm on his bundle, which lay beside him, and contained his necessaries whilst on the travel, and was gazing with looks full of longing down into the valley. Then he plucked some of the flowers which grew among the grass within reach of him and tossed them into the air towards the glorious sunset; afterwards he sat gazing sadly before him, and the burning tears gathered in his eyes. At length he raised his head, and spreading out his arms as if about to embrace some one dear to him, he sang in a clear and very pleasant voice the following song:—

My eyes now rest once more
On thee, O home, sweet home!
My true and honest heart
Has ne'er forgotten thee.
O rosy glow of evening come,
I fain would naught but roses see.

Ye sweetest buds and flowers of love,
Bend down and touch my heart
With winsome sweet caresses.
O swelling bosom, wilt thou burst?
Yet hold in pain and sweet joy fast.
O golden evening red!
O beauteous ray, be my sweet messenger,
And bear to her my sighs and tears —
My tears and sighs on faithfully to her.
And were I now to die,
And roses then did ask thee — say,
"His heart with love — it pined away."

Having sung this song, Frederick took a little piece of wax out of his bundle, warmed it in his bosom, and began in a neat and artistic manner to model a beautiful rose with scores of delicate petals. Whilst busy with this work he hummed to himself some of the lines of the song he had just sung, and so deeply absorbed was he in his occupation that he did not observe the handsome youth who had been standing behind him for some time and attentively watching his work.

"Marry, my friend," began now the youth, "by my troth, that is a dainty piece of work you are making there." Frederick looked round in alarm; but when he looked into the dark friendly eyes of the young stranger, he felt as if he had known him for a long time. Smiling, he replied, "Oh! my dear sir, how can you notice such trifling? it only serves me for pastime on my journey." "Well then," went on the stranger youth, "if you call that delicately formed flower, which is so faithful a reproduction of Nature, trifling, you must be a skilful practised modeller. You have afforded me a pleasant surprise in two ways. First, I was quite touched to the heart by the song you sang so admirably to Martin Häscher's Zarte Buchstabenweis ; and now I cannot but admire your artistic skill in modelling. How much farther do you intend to travel today?" Frederick replied, "Yonder lies the goal of my journey before our eyes. I am going home, to the famed imperial town of Nuremberg. But as the sun has now been set some time, I shall pass the night in the village below there, and then by being up and away in the early morning I can be in Nuremberg at noon." "Marry," cried the youth, delighted, "how finely things will fit; we are both going the same way, for I want to go to Nuremberg. I will spend the night with you here in the village, and then we'll proceed on our way again tomorrow. And now let us talk a little." The youth, Reinhold by name, threw himself down beside Frederick on the grass, and continued, "If I mistake not, you are a skilful artist-caster, are you not? I infer it from your style of modelling; or perhaps you are a worker in gold and silver?" Frederick cast down his eyes sadly, and said dejectedly, "Marry, my dear sir, you are taking me for something far better and higher than I really am. Well, I will speak candidly; I have learned the trade of a cooper, and am now going to work for a well-known master in Nuremberg. You will no doubt look down upon me with contempt since, instead of being able to mould and cast splendid statues, and such like, all I can do is to hoop casks and tubs." Reinhold burst out laughing, and cried, "Now that I call droll. I shall look down upon you — eh? because you are a cooper; why man, that's what I am; I'm nothing but a cooper." Frederick opened his eyes wide in astonishment; he did not know what to make of it, for Reinhold's dress was in keeping with anything sooner than a journeyman cooper's on travel. His doublet of fine black cloth, trimmed with slashed velvet, his dainty ruff, his short broadsword, and baretta with a long drooping feather, seemed rather to point to a prosperous merchant; and yet again there was a strange something about the face and form of the youth which completely negatived the idea of a merchant. Reinhold, noticing Frederick's doubting glances, undid his travelling-bundle and produced his cooper's apron and knife-belt, saying, "Look here, my friend, look here. Have you any doubts now as to my being a comrade? I perceive you are astonished at my clothing, but I have just come from Strasburg, where the coopers go about the streets as fine as noblemen. Certainly I did once set my heart upon something else like you, but now to be a cooper is the topmost height of my ambition, and I have staked many a grand hope upon it. Is it not the same with you, comrade? But I could almost believe that a dark cloud-shadow had been hung unawares about the brightness of your youth, so that you are no longer able to look freely and gladly about you. The song which you were just singing was full of pain and of the yearning of love; but there were strains in it that seemed as if they proceeded from my own heart, and I somehow fancy I know all that is locked up within your breast. You may therefore all the more put confidence in me, for shall we not then be good comrades in Nuremberg?" Reinhold threw his arm around Frederick and looked kindly into his eyes. Whereupon Frederick said, "The more I look at you, honest friend, the stronger I feel drawn towards you; I clearly discern within my breast the wonderful voice which faithfully echoes the cry that you are a sympathetic spirit I must tell you all — not that a poor fellow like me has any important secrets to confide to you, but simply because there is room in the heart of the true friend for his friend's pain, and during the first moments of our new acquaintance even I acknowledge you to be my truest friend.

"I am now a cooper, and may boast that I understand my work; but all my thoughts have been directed to another and a nobler art since my very childhood. I wished to become a great master in casting statues and in silver-work, like Peter Fischer1 or the Italian Benvenuto Cellini;2 and so I worked with intense ardour along with Herr Johannes Holzschuer,3 the well-known worker in silver in my native town yonder. For although he did not exactly cast statues himself, he was yet able to give me a good introduction to the art. And Herr Tobias Martin, the master-cooper, often came to Herr Holzschuer's with his daughter, pretty Rose. Without being consciously aware of it, I fell in love with her. I then left home and went to Augsburg in order to learn properly the art of casting, but this first caused my smouldering passion to burst out into flames. I saw and heard nothing but Rose; every exertion and all labour that did not tend to the winning of her grew hateful to me. And so I adopted the only course that would bring me to this goal. For Master Martin will only give his daughter to the cooper who shall make the very best masterpiece in his house, and who of course finds favour in his daughter's eyes as well. I deserted my own art to learn cooperage. I am now going to Nuremberg to work for Master Martin. But now that my home lies before me and Rose's image rises up before my eyes, I feel overcome with anxiety and nervousness, and my heart sinks within me. Now I see clearly how foolishly I have acted; for I don't even know whether Rose loves me or whether she ever will love me." Reinhold had listened to Frederick's story with increasing attention. He now rested his head on his arm, and, shading his eyes with his hand, asked in a hollow moody voice, "And has Rose never given you any signs of her love?" "Nay," replied Frederick, "nay, for when I left Nuremberg she was more a child than a maiden. No doubt she liked me; she smiled upon me most sweetly when I never wearied plucking flowers for her in Herr Holzschuer's garden and weaving them into wreaths, but ——" "Oh! then all hope is not yet lost," cried Reinhold suddenly, and so vehemently and in such a disagreeably shrill voice that Frederick was almost terrified. At the same time he leapt to his feet, his sword rattling against his side, and as he stood upright at his full stature the deep shadows of the night fell upon his pale face and distorted his gentle features in a most unpleasant way, so

39

that Frederick cried, perfectly alarmed, "What's happened to you all at once?" and stepping back, his foot knocked against Reinhold's bundle. There proceeded from it the jarring of some stringed instrument, and Reinhold cried angrily, "You ill-mannered fellow, don't break my lute all to pieces." The instrument was fastened to the bundle; Reinhold unbuckled it and ran his fingers wildly over the strings as if he would break them all. But his playing soon grew soft and melodious. "Come, brother," said he in the same gentle tone as before, "let us now go down into the village. I've got a good means here in my hands to banish the evil spirits who may cross our path, and who might in particular have any dealings with me." "Why, brother," replied Frederick, "what evil spirits will be likely to have anything to do with us on the way? But your playing is very, very nice; please go on with it."

The golden stars were beginning to dot the dark azure sky. The night breezes in low murmurous whispers swept lightly over the fragrant meadows. The brooks babbled louder, and the trees rustled in the distant woods round about Then Frederick and Reinhold went down the slope playing and singing, and the sweet notes of their songs, so full of noble aspirations, swelled up clear and sharp in the air, as if they had been plumed arrows of light. Arrived at their quarters for the night, Reinhold quickly threw aside lute and bundle and strained Frederick to his heart; and Frederick felt on his cheeks the scalding tears which Reinhold shed.

1 Peter Vischer (c. 1455–1529), a native of Nuremberg, one of the most distinguished of German sculptors, was chiefly engaged in making monuments for deceased princes in various parts of Germany and central Europe. The shrine in St. Sebald's, mentioned above, is generally considered his masterpiece.

2 Benvenuto Cellini (1500–1569) of Florence, goldsmith and worker in metals. Mr. W. M. Rossetti rightly says that his biography, written by himself, forms one of the most "fascinating" of books. It has been translated into English by Thomas Roscoe, and by Goethe into German.

3 Holzschuher was the name of an old and important family in Nuremberg. Fifty-four years before the date of the present story, that is in 1526, a member of the family was burgomaster of his native town, and was painted by Dürer.

How the two young journeymen, Reinhold and Frederick, were taken into Master Martin's house.

Next morning when Frederick awoke he missed his new-won friend, who had the night before thrown himself down upon the straw pallet at his side; and as his lute and his bundle were likewise missing, Frederick quite concluded that Reinhold, from reasons which were unknown to him, had left him and gone another road. But directly he stepped out of the house Reinhold came to meet him, his bundle on his back and his lute under his arm, and dressed altogether differently from what he had been the day before. He had taken the feather out of his baretta, and laid aside his sword, and had put on a plain burgher's doublet of an unpretentious colour, instead of the fine one with the velvet trimmings. "Now, brother," he cried, laughing merrily to his astonished friend, "you will acknowledge me for your true comrade and faithful work-mate now, eh? But let me tell you that for a youth in love you have slept most soundly. Look how high the sun is. Come, let us be going on our way." Frederick was silent and busied with his own thoughts; he scarcely answered Reinhold's questions and scarcely heeded his jests. Reinhold, however, was full of exuberant spirits; he ran from side to side, shouted, and waved his baretta in the air. But he too became more and more silent the nearer they approached the town. "I can't go any farther, I am so full of nervousness and anxiety and sweet sadness; let us rest a little while beneath these trees." Thus spake Frederick just before they reached the gate; and he threw himself down quite exhausted in the grass. Reinhold sat down beside him, and after a while began, "I daresay you thought me extremely strange yesterday evening, good brother mine. But as you told me about your love, and were so very dejected, then all kinds of foolish nonsense flooded my mind and made me quite confused, and would have made me mad in the end if your good singing and my lute had not driven away the evil spirits. But this morning when the first ray of sunlight awoke me, all my gaiety of heart returned, for all nasty feelings had already left me last evening. I ran out, and whilst wandering among the undergrowth a crowd of fine things came into my mind: how I had found you, and how all my heart felt drawn towards you. There also occurred to me a pretty little story which happened some time ago when I was in Italy; I will tell it to you, since it is a remarkable illustration of what true friendship can do.

"It chanced that a noble prince, a warm patron and friend of the Fine Arts, offered a very large prize for a painting, the subject of which was definitely fixed, and which, though a splendid subject, was one difficult to treat. Two young painters, united by the closest bond of friendship and wont to work together, resolved to compete for the prize. They communicated their designs to each other and had long talks as to how they should overcome the difficulties connected with the subject. The elder, more experienced in drawing and in arrangement and grouping, had soon formed a conception of the picture and sketched it; then he went to the younger, whom he found so discouraged in the very designing that he would have given the scheme up, had not the elder constantly encouraged him, and imparted to him good advice. But when they began to paint, the younger, a master in colour, was able to give his friend many a hint, which he turned to the best account; and eventually it was found that the younger had never designed a better picture, nor the elder coloured one better. The pieces being finished, the two artists fell upon each other's neck; each was delighted, enraptured, with the other's work, and each adjudged the prize, which they both deserved, to his friend. But when, eventually, the prize was declared to have fallen to the younger, he cried, ashamed, 'Oh! how can I have gained the prize? What is my merit in comparison with that of my friend? I should never have produced anything at all good without his advice and valuable assistance.' Then said the elder, 'And did not you too stand by me with invaluable counsel? My picture is certainly not bad; but yours has carried off the prize as it deserved. To strive honestly and openly towards the same goal, that is the way of true friends; the wreath which the victor wins confers honour also upon the vanquished. I love you now all the more that you have so bravely striven, and in your victory I also reap fame and honour.' And the painter was right, was he not, Frederick? Honest contention for the same prize, without any malicious reserve, ought to unite true friends still more and knit their hearts still closer, instead of setting them at variance. Ought there to be any room in noble minds for petty envy or malicious hate?" "Never, certainly not," replied Frederick. "We are now faithful loving brothers, and shall both in a short time construct our masterpiece in Nuremburg, a good two-tun cask, made without fire; but Heaven forbid that I should feel the least spark of envy if yours, dear brother Reinhold, turned out to be better than mine." "Ha! ha! ha!" laughed Reinhold heartily, "go on with you and your masterpiece; you'll soon manage that to the joy of all good coopers. And let me tell you that in all that concerns calculation of size and proportion, and drawing plans of sections of circles, you'll find I'm your man. And then in choosing your wood you may rely fully upon me. Staves of the holm oak felled in winter, without worm-holes, without either red or white streaks, and without blemish, that's what we must look for; you may trust my eyes. I will stand by you with all the help I can, in both deed and counsel; and my own masterpiece will be none the worse for it." "But in the name of all that's holy," broke in Frederick here, "why are we chattering about who is to make the best masterpiece? Are we to have any contest about the matter?— the best masterpiece — to gain Rose! What are we thinking about? The very thought makes me giddy." "Marry, brother," cried Reinhold, still laughing, "there was no thought at all of Rose. You are a dreamer. Come along, let us go on if we are to get into the town." Frederick leapt to his feet, and went on his way, his mind in a whirl of confusion.

As they were washing and brushing off the dust of travel in the hostelry, Reinhold said to Frederick, "To tell you the truth, I for my part don't know for what master I shall work;

I have no acquaintances here at all; and I thought you would perhaps take me along with you to Master Martin's, brother? Perhaps I may get taken on by him." "You remove a heavy load from my heart," replied Frederick, "for if you will only stay with me, it will be easier for me to conquer my anxiety and nervousness." And so the two young apprentices trudged sturdily on to the house of the famed cooper, Master Martin.

It happened to be the very Sunday on which Master Martin gave his feast in honour of his election as "Candle-master;" and the two arrived just as they were partaking of the good cheer. So it was that as Reinhold and Frederick entered into Master Martin's house they heard the ringing of glasses and the confused buzz and rattle of a merry company at a feast. "Oh!" said Frederick quite cast down, "we have, it seems, come at an unseasonable time." "Nay, I think we have come exactly at the right time," replied Reinhold, "for Master Martin is sure to be in good humour after a good feast, and well disposed to grant our wishes." They caused their arrival to be announced to Master Martin, and soon he appeared in the entrance-passage, dressed in holiday garb and with no small amount of colour in his nose and on his cheeks. On catching sight of Frederick he cried, "Holla! Frederick, my good lad, have you come home again? That's fine! And so you have taken up the best of all trades — cooperage. Herr Holzschuer cuts confounded wry faces when your name is mentioned, and says a great artist is ruined in you, and that you could have cast little images and espaliers as fine as those in St. Sebald's or on Fugger's1 house at Augsburg. But that's all nonsense; you have done quite right to step across the way here. Welcome, lad, welcome with all my heart." And therewith Herr Martin took him by the shoulders and drew him to his bosom, as was his wont, thoroughly well pleased. This kind reception by Master Martin infused new spirits into Frederick; all his nervousness left him, so that unhesitatingly and without constraint he was able not only to prefer his own request but also warmly to recommend Reinhold. "Well, to tell you the truth," said Master Martin, "you could not have come at a more fortunate time than just now, for work keeps increasing and I am bankrupt of workmen. You are both heartily welcome. Put your bundles down and come in; our meal is indeed almost finished, but you can come and take your seats at the table, and Rose shall look after you and get you something." And Master Martin and the two journeymen went into the room. There sat the honest masters, the worthy syndic Jacobus Paumgartner at their head, all with hot red faces. Dessert was being served, and a better brand of wine was sparkling in the glasses. Every master was talking about something different from all his neighbours and in a loud voice, and yet they all thought they understood each other; and now and again some of them burst out in a hearty laugh without exactly knowing why. When, however. Master Martin came back, leading the two young men by the hand, and announced aloud that he brought two journeymen who had come to him well provided with testimonials just at the time he wanted them, then all grew silent, each master scrutinising the smart young fellows with

a smile of comfortable satisfaction, whilst Frederick cast his
eyes down and twisted his baretta about in his hands. Master
Martin directed the youths to places at the very bottom of
the table; but these were soon the very best of all, for Rose
came and took her seat between the two, and served them
attentively both with dainty dishes and with good rich
wine. There was Rose, a most winsome picture of grace and
loveliness, seated between the two handsome youths, all
in midst of the bearded old men — it was a right pleasant
sight to see; the mind instantly recalled a bright morning
cloud rising solitary above the dim dark horizon, or beautiful
spring flowers lifting up their bright heads from amidst the
uniform colourless grass. Frederick was so very happy and
so very delighted that his breath almost failed him for joy;
and only now and again did he venture to steal a glance at
her who filled his heart so fully. His eyes were fixedly bent
upon his plate; how could he possibly dream of eating the
least morsel? Reinhold, on the other hand, could not turn
his sparkling, radiant eyes away from the lovely maiden. He
began to talk about his long journeys in such a wonderful
way that Rose had never heard anything like it. She seemed
to see everything of which he spoke rise up vividly before
her in manifold ever-changing forms. She was all eyes and
ears; and when Reinhold, carried away by the fire of his own
words, grasped her hand and pressed it to his heart, she didn't
know where she was. "But bless me," broke off Reinhold all
at once, "why, Frederick, you are quite silent and still. Have
you lost your tongue? Come, let us drink to the weal of the

lovely maiden who has so hospitably entertained us." With a trembling hand Frederick seized the huge drinking-glass that Reinhold had filled to the brim and now insisted on his draining to the last drop. "Now here's long life to our excellent master," cried Reinhold, again filling the glasses and again compelling Frederick to empty his. Then the fiery juices of the wine permeated his veins and stirred up his stagnant blood until it coursed as it were triumphantly through his every limb. "Oh! I feel so indescribably happy," he whispered, the burning blushes mounting into his cheeks. "Oh! I have never felt so happy in all my life before." Rose, who undoubtedly gave another interpretation to his words, smiled upon him with incomparable gentleness. Then, quit of all his embarrassing shyness, Frederick said, "Dear Rose, I suppose you no longer remember me, do you?" "But, dear Frederick," replied Rose, casting down her eyes, "how could I possibly forget you in so short a time? When you were at Herr Holzschuer's — true, I was only a mere child then, yet you did not disdain to play with me, and always had something nice and pretty to talk about. And that dear little basket made of fine silver wire that you gave me at Christmas-time, I've got it still, and I take care of it and keep it as a precious memento." Frederick was intoxicated with delight and tears glittered in his eyes. He tried to speak, but there only burst from his breast, like a deep sigh, the words, "O Rose — dear, dear Rose." "I have always really from my heart longed to see you again," went on Rose; "but that you would become a cooper, that I never for a moment dreamed. Oh! when I call to mind the beautiful things that you made whilst you were with Master Holzschuer — oh! it really is a pity that you have not stuck to your art." "O Rose," said Frederick, "it is only for your sake that I have become unfaithful to it." No sooner had he uttered these words than he could have sunk into the earth for shame and confusion. He had most thoughtlessly let the confession slip over his lips. Rose, as if divining all, turned her face away from him; whilst he in vain struggled for words.

Then Herr Paumgartner struck the table a bang with his knife, and announced to the company that Herr Vollrad, a worthy Meistersinger ,2 would favour them with a song. Herr Vollrad at once rose to his feet, cleared his throat, and sang such an excellent song in the Güldne Tonweis 3 of Herr Vogelgesang that everybody's heart leapt with joy, and even Frederick recovered himself from his awkward embarrassment again. After Herr Vollrad had sung several other excellent songs to several other excellent tunes, such as the Süsser Ton , the Krummzinkenweis , the Geblümte Paradiesweis , the Frisch Pomeranzenweis , &c., he called upon any one else at the table who understood anything of the sweet and delectable art of the Meistersinger also to honour them with a song. Then Reinhold rose to his feet and said that if he might be allowed to accompany himself on his lute in the Italian fashion he would give them a song, keeping, however, strictly to the German tune. As nobody had any objection he fetched his instrument, and, after a little tuneful prelude, began the following song:—

Where is the little fount
Where sparkles the spicy wine?
From forth its golden depths
Its golden sparkles mount
And dance 'fore the gladdened eye.
This beautiful little fount
Wherein the golden wine
Sparkles — who made it,
With thoughtful skill and fine,
With such high art and industry,
That praise deserve so well?
This little fount so gay,
Wrought with high art and fine,
Was fashioned by one
Who ne'er an artist was —
But a brave young cooper he,
His veins with rich wine glowing,
His heart with true love singing,
And ever lovingly —
For that's young cooper's way
In all the things he does.

This song pleased them all down to the ground, but none more so than Master Martin, whose eyes sparkled with pleasure and delight. Without heeding Vollrad, who had almost too much to say about Hans Müller's Stumpfe Schossweis , which the youth had caught excellently well,— Master Martin, without heeding him, rose from his seat, and, lifting his passglas 4 above his head, called aloud, "Come here, honest cooper and Meistersinger , come here and drain this glass with me, your Master Martin." Reinhold had to do as he was bidden. Returning to his place, he whispered into Frederick's ear, who was looking very pensive, "Now, you must sing — sing the song you sang last night." "Are you mad?" asked Frederick, quite angry. But Reinhold turned to the company and said in a loud voice, "My honoured gentlemen and masters, my dear brother Frederick here can sing far finer songs, and has a much pleasanter voice than I have, but his throat has got full of dust from his travels, and he will treat you to some of his songs another time, and then to the most admirable tunes." And they all began to shower down their praises upon Frederick, as if he had already sung. Indeed, in the end, more than one of the masters was of opinion that his voice was really more agreeable than journeyman Reinhold's, and Herr Vollrad also, after he had drunk another glass, was convinced that Frederick could use the beautiful German tunes far better than Reinhold, for the latter had too much of the Italian style about him. And Master Martin, throwing his head back into his neck, and giving his round belly a hearty slap, cried, "Those are my journeymen, my journeymen, I tell you — mine, master-cooper Tobias Martin's of Nuremberg." And all the other masters nodded their heads in assent, and, sipping the last drops out of the bottom of their tall glasses, said, "Yes, yes. Your brave, honest journeymen, Master Martin — that they are." At length it was time to retire to rest Master Martin led

Reinhold and Frederick each into a bright cheerful room in his own house.

1 The family of Fugger, which rose from the position of poor weavers to be the richest merchant princes in Augsburg, decorated their house with frescoes externally, like so many other old German families.

2 During the fourteenth, fifteenth, and sixteenth centuries there existed in many German towns (Nuremberg, Frankfort, Strasburg, Ulm, Mayence, &c.) associations or guild-like corporations of burghers, the object of which was the cultivation of song in the same systematic way that the mechanical arts were practised. They framed strict and well-defined codes of rules (Tablatures) by means of which they tested a singer's capabilities. As the chief aims which they set before themselves were the invention of new tunes or melodies, and also songs (words), it resulted that they fell into the inevitable vice of cold formalism, and banished the true spirit of poetry by their many arbitrary rules about rhyme, measure, and melody, and the dry business-like manner in which they worked. The guild or company generally consisted of five distinct grades, the ultimate one being that of master, entrance into which was only permitted to the man who had invented a new melody or tune, and had sung it in public without offending against any of the laws of the Tablature . The subjects, which, as the singers were honest burghers, could not be taken from topics in which chivalric life took any interest, were mostly restricted to fables, legendary lore, and consisted very largely of Biblical narratives and passages.

3 *These words are the names of various "tunes," and signified in each case a particular metre, rhyme, melody, &c, so that each was a brief definition of a number of individual items, so to speak. These Meistersinger technical terms (or slang?) are therefore not translatable, nor could they be made intelligible by paraphrase, even if the requisite information for each instance were at hand.*

4 *A glass divided by means of marks placed at intervals from top to bottom. It was usual for one who was invited to drink to drink out of the challenger's glass down to the mark next below the top of the liquid.*

How the third journeyman came into Master Martin's house and what followed in consequence.

After the two journeymen had worked for some weeks in Master Martin's workshop, he perceived that in all that concerned measurement with rule and compass, and calculation, and estimation of measure and size by eyesight, Reinhold could hardly find his match, but it was a different thing when it came to hard work at the bench or with the adze or the mallet. Then Reinhold soon grew tired, and the work did not progress, no matter how great efforts he might make. On the other hand, Frederick planed and hammered away without growing particularly tired. But one thing they had in common with each other, and that was their well-mannered behaviour, marked, principally at Reinhold's instance, by much natural cheerfulness and good-natured enjoyment. Besides, even when hard at work, they did not spare their throats, especially when pretty Rose was present, but sang many an excellent song, their pleasant voices harmonising well together. And whenever Frederick, glancing shyly across at Rose, seemed to be falling into his melancholy mood, Reinhold at once struck up a satirical song that he composed, beginning, "The cask is not the cither, nor is the cither the cask," so that old Herr Martin often had to let the croze-adze which he had raised, sink again without striking and hold his big belly as it wabbled from his internal laughter. Above all, the two journeymen, and mainly Reinhold, had completely won their way into Martin's favour; and it was not difficult to observe that Rose found a good many pretexts for lingering oftener and longer in the workshop than she certainly otherwise would have done.

One day Master Martin entered his open workshop outside the town-gate, where work was carried on all the summer through, with his brow weighted with thought Reinhold and Frederick were in the act of setting up a small cask. Then Master Martin planted himself before them with his arms crossed over his chest and said, "I can't tell you how pleased I am with you, my good journeymen, but I am just now in a great difficulty. They write me from the Rhine that this will be a more prosperous wine-year than there ever has been before. A learned man says that the comet which has been seen in the heavens will fructify the earth with its wonderful tail, so that the glowing heat which fabricates the precious metals down in the deepest mines will all stream upwards and evaporate into the thirsty vines, till they prosper and thrive and put forth multitudes of grapes, and the liquid fire with which they are filled will be poured out into the grapes. It will be almost three hundred years before such a favourable constellation occurs again. So now we shall all have our hands full of work. And then there's his Lordship the Bishop of Bamberg has written to me and ordered a large cask. That we can't get done; and I shall have to look about for another useful journeyman. Now I should not like to take the first fellow I meet off the street amongst us, and yet the matter is very urgent. If you know of a good journeyman anywhere whom you would be willing to work with, you have only to tell me, and I will get him here, even though it should cost me a good sum of money."

Hardly had Master Martin finished speaking when a young man, tall and stalwart, shouted to him in a loud voice, "Hi! you there! is this Master Martin's workshop?" "Certainly," replied Master Martin, going towards the young man, "certainly it is; but you needn't shout so deuced loud and lumber in like that; that's not the way to find people." "Ha! ha! ha!" laughed the young fellow, "marry, you are Master Martin himself, for — fat belly — stately double-chin — sparkling eyes, and red nose — yes, that's just how he was described to me. I bid you good hail, Master Martin." "Well, and what do you want from Master Martin?" he asked, indignantly. The young fellow replied, "I am a journeyman cooper, and merely wanted to ask if I could find work with you." Marvelling that just as he was thinking about looking out for a journeyman one should come to him like this, Master Martin drew back a few paces and eyed the young man from head to foot. He, however, met the scrutiny unabashed and with sparkling eyes. Noting his broad chest, stalwart build, and powerful arms, Master Martin thought within himself, it's just such a lusty fellow as this that I want, and he at once asked him for his trade testimonials.1 "I haven't them with me just at this present moment," replied the young man, "but I will get them in a short time; and I give you now my word of honour that I will work well and honestly, and that must suffice you." Thereupon, without waiting for Master Martin's reply, the young journeyman stepped into the workshop. He threw down his baretta and bundle, took off his doublet, put on his apron, and said, "Come, Master Martin, tell me at once what I am to begin with." Master Martin, completely taken aback by the young stranger's resolute vigour and promptitude, had to think a little; then he said, "Come then, my fine fellow, and show me at once that you are a good cooper; take this croze-adze and finish the groove of that cask lying in the vice yonder." The stranger performed what he had been bidden with remarkable strength, quickness, and skill; and then he cried, laughing loudly, "Now, Master Martin, have you any doubts now as to my being a good cooper? But," he continued, going backwards and forwards through the shop, and examining the instruments and tools, and supply of wood, "but though you are well supplied with useful stores and — but what do you call this little thing of a mallet? I suppose it's for your children to play with; and this little adze here — why it must be for your apprentices when they first begin," and he swung round his head the huge heavy mallet which Reinhold could not lift and which Frederick had great difficulty in wielding; and then he did the same with the ponderous adze with which Master Martin himself worked. Then he rolled a couple of huge casks on one side as if they had been light balls, and seized one of the large thick beams which had not yet been worked at "Marry, master," he cried, "marry, this is good sound oak; I wager it will snap like glass." And thereupon he struck the stave against the grindstone so that it broke clean in half with a loud crack. "Pray be so kind," said Master Martin, "pray have the kindness, my good fellow, to kick that two-tun cask about or to pull down the whole shop. There, you can take that balk for a mallet, and that you may have an adze to your mind I will have Roland's sword, which is three yards long, fetched for you from the town-house." "Ay, do, that's just the thing," said the young man, his eyes flashing; but the next minute he cast them down upon the ground and said, lowering his voice, "I only thought, good master, that you wanted right strong journeymen for your heavy work, and now I have, I see, been too forward, too swaggering, in displaying my bodily strength. But do take me on to work, I will faithfully do whatever you shall require of me." Master Martin scanned the youth's features, and could not but admit that he had never seen more nobility and at the same time more downright honesty in any man's face. And yet, as he looked upon the young fellow, there stole into his mind a dim recollection of some man whom he had long esteemed and honoured, but he could not clearly call to mind who it was. For this reason he granted the young man's request on the spot, only enjoining upon him to produce at the earliest opportunity the needful credible trade attestations.

Meanwhile Reinhold and Frederick had finished setting up their cask and were now busy driving on the first hoops. Whilst doing this they were always in the habit of striking up a song; and on this occasion they began a good song in Adam Puschmann's Stieglitzweis . Then Conrad (that was the name of the new journeyman) shouted across from the bench where Master Martin had placed him, "By my troth, what squalling do you call that? I could fancy I hear mice squeaking somewhere about the shop. An you mean to sing at all, sing so that it will cheer the heart and make the work go down well. That's how I sing a bit now and again." And he began to bellow out a noisy hunting ditty with its hollas! and hoy, boys! and he imitated the yelping of the hounds and the shrill shouts of the hunters in such a clear, keen, stentorian voice that the huge casks rang again and all the workshop echoed. Master Martin held his hands over his ears, and Dame Martha's (Valentine's widow) little boys, who were playing in the shop, crept timorously behind the piled-up staves. Just at this moment Rose came in, amazed, nay, frightened at the terrible noise; it could not be called singing anyhow. As soon as Conrad observed her, he at once stopped, and leaving his bench he approached her and greeted her with the most polished grace. Then he said in a gentle voice, whilst an ardent fire gleamed in his bright brown eyes, "Lovely lady, what a sweet rosy light shone into this humble workman's hut when you came in! Oh! had I but perceived you sooner, I had not outraged your tender ears with my wild hunting ditty." Then, turning to Master Martin and the other journeymen, he cried, "Oh! do stop your abominable knocking and rattling. As long as this gracious lady honours us with her presence, let mallets and drivers rest. Let us only listen to her sweet voice, and with bowed head hearken to what she may command us, her humble servants." Reinhold and Frederick looked at each other utterly amazed; but Master Martin burst out laughing and said, "Well, Conrad, it is now plain that you are the most ridiculous donkey who ever put on apron. First you come here and want to break everything to pieces like an uncultivated giant; then you bellow in such a way as to make our ears tingle; and, as a fitting climax to all your foolishness, you take my little daughter Rose for a lady of rank and act like a love-smitten Junker." Conrad replied, coolly, "Your lovely daughter I know very well, my worthy Master Martin; but I tell you that she is the most peerless lady who treads the earth, and if Heaven grant it she would honour the very noblest of Junkers by permitting him to be her Paladin in faithful knightly love." Master Martin held his sides, and it was only by giving vent to his laughter in hums and haws that he prevented himself from choking. As soon as he could at all speak, he stammered, "Good, very good, my most excellent youth; you may continue to regard my daughter as a lady of high rank, I shall not hinder you; but, irrespective of that, will you have the goodness to go back to your bench?" Conrad stood as if spell-bound, his eyes cast down upon the ground; and rubbing his forehead, he said in a low voice, "Ay, it is so," and did as he was bidden. Rose, as she always did in the shop, sat down upon a small cask, which Frederick placed for her, and which Reinhold carefully dusted. At Master Martin's express desire they again struck up the admirable song in which they had been so rudely interrupted by Conrad's bluster; but he went on with his work at the bench, quite still, and entirely wrapped up in his own thoughts.

When the song came to an end Master Martin said,

"Heaven has endowed you with a noble gift, my brave lads; you would not believe how highly I value the delectable art of song. Why, once I wanted to be a Meistersinger myself, but I could not manage it, even though I tried all I knew how. All that I gained by my efforts was ridicule and mockery. In 'Voluntary Singing'2 I either got into false 'appendages,' or 'double notes,' or a wrong 'measure,' or an unsuitable 'embellishment,' or started the wrong melody altogether. But you will succeed better, and it shall be said, what the master can't do, his journeymen can. Next Sunday after the sermon there will be a singing contest by the Meistersinger at the usual time in St. Catherine's Church. But before the 'Principal Singing' there will be a 'Voluntary,' in which you may both of you win praise and honour in your beautiful art, for any stranger who can sing at all, may freely take part in this. And, he! Conrad, my journeyman Conrad," cried Master Martin across to the bench, "would not you also like to get into the singing-desk and treat our good folk to your fine hunting-chorus?" Without looking up, Conrad replied, "Mock not, good master, mock not; everything in its place. Whilst you are being edified by the Meistersinger , I shall enjoy myself in my own way on the Allerwiese."

And what Master Martin anticipated came to pass. Reinhold got into the singing-desk and sang divers songs to divers tunes, with which all the Meistersingers were well pleased; and although they were of opinion that the singer had not made any mistake, yet they had a slight objection to urge against him — a sort of something foreign about his style, but yet they could not say exactly in what it consisted. Soon afterwards Frederick took his seat in the singing-desk; and doffing his baretta, he stood some seconds looking silently before him; then after sending a glance at the audience which entered lovely Rose's bosom like a burning arrow, and caused her to fetch a deep sigh, he began such a splendid song in Heinrich Frauenlob's3 Zarter Ton , that all the masters agreed with one accord there was none amongst them who could surpass the young journeyman.

The singing-school came to an end towards evening, and Master Martin, in order to finish off the day's enjoyment in proper style, betook himself in high good-humour to the Allerwiese along with Rose. The two journeymen, Reinhold and Frederick, were permitted to accompany them; Rose was walking between them. Frederick, radiant with delight at the masters' praise, and intoxicated with happiness, ventured to breathe many a daring word in Rose's ear which she, however, casting down her eyes in maidenly coyness, pretended not to hear. Rather she turned to Reinhold, who, according to his wont, was running on with all sorts of merry nonsense; nor did he hesitate to place his arm in Rose's. Whilst even at a considerable distance from the Allerwiese they could hear noisy shouts and cries. Arrived at the place where the young men were amusing themselves in all kinds of games, partly chivalric, they heard the crowd shout time after time, "Won again! won again! He's the strongest again! Nobody can compete with him." Master Martin, on working his way through the crowd, perceived that it was nobody else but his journeyman Conrad who was reaping all this praise and exciting the people to all this applause. He had beaten everybody in racing and boxing and throwing the spear. As Martin came up, Conrad was shouting out and inquiring if there was anybody who would have a merry bout with him with blunt swords. This challenge several stout young patricians, well accustomed to this species of pastime, stepped forward and accepted. But it was not long before Conrad had again, without much trouble or exertion, overcome all his opponents; and the applause at his skill and strength seemed as if it would never end.

The sun had set; the last glow of evening died away, and twilight began to creep on apace. Master Martin, with Rose and the two journeymen, had thrown themselves down beside a babbling spring of water. Reinhold was telling of the wonders of distant Italy, but Frederick, quiet and happy, had his eyes fixed on pretty Rose's face. Then Conrad drew near with slow hesitating steps, as if rather undecided in his own mind whether he should join them or not Master Martin called to him, "Come along, Conrad, come along, come along; you have borne yourself bravely on the meadow; that's what I like in my journeymen, and it's what becomes them. Don't be shy, lad; come and join us, you have my permission." Conrad cast a withering glance at his master, who however met it with a condescending nod; then the young journeyman said moodily, "I am not the least bit shy of you, and I have not asked your permission whether I may lie down here or not,— in fact, I have not come to you at all. All my opponents I have stretched in the sand in the merry knightly sports, and all I now wanted was to ask this lovely lady whether she would not honour me with the beautiful flowers she wears in her bosom, as the prize of the chivalric contest." Therewith he dropped upon one knee in front of Rose, and looked her straight and honestly in the face with his clear brown eyes, and he begged, "O give me those beautiful flowers, sweet Rose, as the prize of victory; you cannot refuse me that." Rose at once took the flowers from her bosom and gave them to him, laughing and saying, "Ay, I know well that a brave knight like you deserves a token of honour from a lady; and so here, you may have my withered flowers." Conrad kissed the flowers that were given him, and then fastened them in his baretta; but Master Martin, rising to his feet, cried, "There's another of your silly tricks — come, let us be going home; it is getting dark." Herr Martin strode on first; Conrad with modest courtly grace took Rose's arm; whilst Reinhold and Frederick followed them considerably out of humour. People who met them, stopped and turned round to look after them, saying, "Marry, look now, look; that's the rich cooper Thomas Martin, with his pretty little daughter and his stout journeymen. A fine set of people I call them."

1 These would consist of the certificate of his admission into the ranks of the journeymen of the guild, of the certificates of proper dismissal signed by the various masters for whom he had worked whilst on travel, together with testimonials of good conduct from the same masters.

2 *On these great singing days, generally on Sundays in the churches, and on special occasions in the town-house, the "performances" consisted of three parts. 1. First came a "Voluntary Solo–Singing," in which anybody, even a stranger, might participate, no contest being entered into, and no rewards given. 2. This was followed by a song by all the masters in chorus, 3. Then came the "Principal Singing," the chief "event" of the day — the actual singing contest. Four judges were appointed to examine those who successively presented themselves, being guided by the strict laws and regulations of the Tablatures . Those who violated these laws, that is, who made mistakes, had to leave the singing-desk; the successful ones were, however, crowned with wreaths, and had earned the right to act themselves as judges on future occasions.*

3 *Heinrich von Meissen, called Frauenlob (died 1318), after having lived at various courts in both the north and the south of Germany, settled at Mayence and gathered together (1311) a school or society of burgher singers.*

Of Dame Martha's conversation with Rose about the three journeymen, Conrad's quarrel with Master Martin.

Generally it is the morning following a holiday when young girls are wont to enjoy all the pleasure of it, and taste it, and thoroughly digest it; and this after celebration they seem to like far better than the actual holiday itself. And so next morning pretty Rose sat alone in her room with her hands folded on her lap, and her head bent slightly forward in meditation — her spindle and embroidery meanwhile resting. Probably she was now listening to Reinhold's and Frederick's songs, and now watching Conrad cleverly gaining the victory over his competitors, and now she saw him coming to her for the prize of victory; and then she hummed a few lines of a pretty song, and then she whispered, "Do you want my flowers?" whereat a deeper crimson suffused her cheeks, and brighter glances made their way through her downcast eyelashes, and soft sighs stole forth from her inmost heart. Then Dame Martha came in, and Rose was delighted to be able to tell at full length all that had taken place in St. Catherine's Church and on the Allerwiese. When Rose had done speaking, Dame Martha said, smiling, "Oh! so now, dear Rose, you will soon have to make your choice between your three handsome lovers." "For God's sake," burst out Rose, quite frightened, and flushing hotly all over her face, "for mercy's sake, Dame Martha, what do you mean by that? I— three lovers!" "Don't take on so," went on Dame Martha, "don't take on in that way, dear Rose, as if you knew

67

nothing, as if you could guess nothing. Why, where do you put your eyes, girl? you must be quite blind not to see that our journeymen. Reinhold, Frederick, and Conrad — yes, all three of them — are madly in love with you." "What a fancy, to be sure, Dame Martha," whispered Rose, holding her hands before her face. Then Dame Martha knelt down before her, and threw her arm about her, saying, "Come, my pretty, bashful child, take your hands away, and look me straight in the eyes, and then tell me you have not long ago perceived that you fill both the heart and the mind of each of our journeymen, deny that if you can. Nay, I tell you, you can't do it; and it would, i' faith, be a truly wonderful thing if a maiden's eyes did not see a thing of that sort. Why, when you go into the shop, their eyes are off their work and flying across to you in a minute, and they bustle and stir about with new life. And Reinhold and Frederick begin their best songs, and even wild Conrad grows quiet and gentle; each tries to invent some excuse to approach nearer to you, and when you honour one of them with a sweet look or a kindly word, how his eyes sparkle, and his face flushes! Come now, my pet, is it not nice to have such handsome fellows all making love to you? But whether you will choose one of the three or which it will be, that I cannot indeed say, for you are good and kind to them all alike, and yet — and yet — but I must not say more. Now an you come to me and said, 'O Dame Martha, give me your advice, to which of these young men, who are all wanting me, shall I give my hand and heart?' then I should of course answer, 'If your heart does not speak out loudly and distinctly. It's this or it's that, why, let them all three go.' I must say Reinhold pleases me right well, and so does Frederick, and so does Conrad; and then again on the other hand I have something to say against each of them. In fact, dear Rose, when I see them working away so bravely, I always think of my poor Valentine; and I must say that, if he could not perhaps produce any better work, there was yet quite a different kind of swing and style in all that he did do. You could see all his heart was in his work; but with these young fellows it always seems to me as if they only worked so, so — as if they had in their heads different things altogether from their work; nay, it almost strikes me as if it were a burden which they have voluntarily taken up, and were now bearing with sturdy courage. Of them all I can get on best with Frederick; he's such a faithful, affectionate fellow. He is the one who seems to belong to us most; I understand all that he says. And then his love for you is so still, and as shy as a good child's; he hardly dares to look at you, and blushes if you only say a single word to him; and that's what I like so much in the dear lad." A tear seemed to glisten in Rose's eye as Dame Martha said this. She stood up, and turning to the window, said, "I like Frederick very much, but you must not pass over Reinhold contemptuously." "I never dreamt of doing so," replied Dame Martha, "for Reinhold is by a long way the handsomest of all. And what eyes he has! And when he looks you through and through with his bright glances — no, it's more than you can endure. And yet there's something so strange and peculiar in his character, it quite makes me shiver at times, and makes me quite afraid of him. When Reinhold is working in the shop, I should think Herr Martin, when he tells him to do this or do that, must always feel as I should if anybody were to put a bright pan in my kitchen all glittering with gold and precious stones, and should bid me use it like any ordinary common pan — why, I should hardly dare to touch it at all. He tells his stories and talks and talks, and it all sounds like sweet music, and you are quite carried away by it, but when I sit down to think seriously about what he has been saying, I find I haven't understood a single word. And then when he now and again jests in the way we do, and I think now he's just like us, then all at once he looks so distinguished that I get really afraid of him. And yet I can't say that he puffs himself up in the way that many of our Junkers or patricians do; no, it's something else altogether different. In a word, it strikes me, by my troth, as if he held intercourse with higher spirits, as if he belonged, in fact, to another world. Conrad is a wild overbearing fellow, and yet there is something confoundedly distinguished about him as well; it doesn't agree with the cooper's apron somehow. And he always acts as if nobody but he had to give orders, and as if the others must obey him. In the short time that he has been here he has got so far that when he bellows at Master Martin in his loud ringing voice, his master generally does what he wishes. But at the same time he is so good-natured and so thoroughly honest that you can't bear ill-will against him; rather, I must say, that in spite of his wildness, I almost like him better than I do Reinhold, for even if he

70

does speak fearfully grand, you can yet understand him very well. I wager he has once been a campaigner, he may say what he likes. That's why he knows so much about arms, and has even got something of knights' ways about him, which doesn't suit him at all badly. Now do tell me, Rose dear, without any ifs and ands, which of the three journeymen you like best?" "Don't ask me such searching questions, dear Dame Martha," answered Rose. "But of this I am quite sure, that Reinhold does not stir up in me the same feelings that he does in you. It's perfectly true, too, that he is altogether different from his equals; and when he talks I could fancy I enter into a beautiful garden full of bright and magnificent flowers and blossoms and fruits, such as are not to be found on earth, and I like to be amongst them. Since Reinhold has been here I see many things in a different light, and lots of things that were once dim and formless in my mind are now so bright and clear that I can easily distinguish them." Dame Martha rose to her feet, and shaking her finger at Rose as she went out of the room, said, "Ah! ah! Rose, so Reinhold is the favourite then? I didn't think it, I didn't even dream it." Rose made answer as she accompanied her as far as the door, "Pray, dear Dame Martha, think nothing, dream nothing, but leave all to the future. What it brings is the will of God, and to that everybody must bow humbly and gratefully."

Meanwhile it was becoming extremely lively in Master Martin's workshop. In order to execute all his orders he had engaged with ordinary labourers and taken in some apprentices, and they all hammered and knocked till the din could be heard far and wide. Reinhold had finished his calculations and measurements for the great cask that was to be built for the Bishop of Bamberg, whilst Frederick and Conrad had set it up so cleverly that Master Martin's heart laughed in his body, and he cried again and again, "Now that I call a grand piece of work; that'll be the best little cask I've ever made — except my masterpiece." Now the three apprentices stood driving the hoops on to the fitted staves, and the whole place rang again with the din of their mallets. Old Valentine was busy plying his draw-knife, and Dame Martha, her two youngest on her knee, sat just behind Conrad, whilst the other wideawake little rascals were shouting and making a noise, tumbling the hoops about, and chasing each other. In fact, there was so much hubbub and so much vigorous hard work going on that hardly anybody noticed old Herr Johannes Holzschuer as he stepped into the shop. Master Martin went to meet him, and politely inquired what he desired. "Why, in the first place," said Holzschuer, "I want to have a look at my dear Frederick again, who is working away so lustily yonder. And then, goodman Master Martin, I want a stout cask for my wine-cellar, which I will ask you to make for me. Why look you, that cask they are now setting up there is exactly the sort of thing I want; you can let me have that, you've only got to name the price." Reinhold, who had grown tired and had been resting a few minutes down in the shop, and was now preparing to ascend the scaffolding again, heard Holzschuer's words and said, turning his head towards the old gentleman, "Marry, my friend Herr Holzschuer, you need not set your heart upon this cask; we are making it for his Lordship the Bishop of Bamberg." Master Martin, his arms folded on his back, his left foot planted forward, his head thrown back in his neck, blinked at the cask and said proudly, "My dear master, you might have seen from the carefully selected wood and the great pains taken in the work that a masterpiece like that was meant for a prince's1 cellar. My journeyman Reinhold has said the truth; don't set your heart on a piece of work like that. But when the vintage is over I will get you a plain strong little cask made, such as will be suitable for your cellar." Old Holzschuer, incensed at Master Martin's pride, replied that his gold pieces weighed just as much as the Bishop of Bamberg's, and that he hoped he could get good work elsewhere for ready money. Master Martin, although fuming with rage, controlled himself with difficulty; he would not by any means like to offend old Herr Holzschuer, who stood so high in the esteem both of the Council and of all the burghers. At this moment Conrad struck mightier blows than ever with his mallet, so that the whole shop rang and cracked; then Master Martin's internal rage boiled over, and he shouted vehemently, "Conrad, you blockhead, what do you mean by striking so blindly and heedlessly? do you mean to break my cask in pieces?" "Ho! ho!" replied Conrad, looking round defiantly at his master, "Ho! ho! my comical little master, and why should I not?" And therewith he dealt such a terrible blow at the cask that the strongest hoop sprang, rattling, and knocked Reinhold down from the narrow plank on the scaffolding; and it was further evident from the hollow echo that a stave had been broken as well. Completely mastered by his furious anger, Master Martin snatched out of Valentine's hand the bar he was shaving, and striding towards the cask, dealt Conrad a good sound stroke with it on the back, shouting, "You cursed dog!" As soon as Conrad felt the blow he wheeled sharply round, and after standing for a moment as if bereft of his senses, his eyes blazed up with fury, he ground his teeth, and screamed, "Struck! struck!" Then at one bound he was down from the scaffolding, had snatched up an adze that lay on the floor, and aimed a powerful stroke at his master; had not Frederick pulled Martin on one side the blow would have split his head; as it was, the adze only grazed his arm, from which, however, the blood at once began to spurt out. Martin, fat and helpless as he was, lost his equilibrium and fell over the bench, at which one of the apprentices was working, into the floor. They all threw themselves upon Conrad, who was frantic, flourishing his bloody adze in the air, and shouting and screaming in a terrible voice, "Let him go to hell! To hell with him!" Hurling them all off with the strength of a giant, he was preparing to deal a second blow at his poor master, who was gasping for breath and groaning on the floor,— a blow that would have completely done for him — when Rose, pale as a corpse with fright, appeared in the shop-door. As soon as Conrad observed her he stood as if turned to a pillar of stone, the adze suspended in the air. Then he threw the tool away from him, struck his hands together upon his chest, and cried in a voice that went to everybody's heart,

"Oh, good God! good God! what have I done?" and away he rushed out of the shop. No one thought of following him.

Now poor Master Martin was after some difficulty lifted up; it was found, however, that the adze had only penetrated into the thick fleshy part of the arm, and the wound could not therefore be called serious. Old Herr Holzschuer, whom Martin had involved with him in his fall, was pulled out from beneath the shavings, and Dame Martha's children, who ceased not to scream and cry over good Father Martin, were appeased as far as that could be done. As for Martin himself, he was quite dazed, and said if only that devil of a bad journeyman had not spoilt his fine cask he should not make much account of the wound.

Sedan chairs were brought for the old gentlemen, for Holzschuer also had bruised himself rather in his fall. He hurled reproaches at a trade in which they employed such murderous tools, and conjured Frederick to come back to his beautiful art of casting and working in the precious metals, and the sooner the better.

As soon as the dusk of evening began to creep up over the sky, Frederick, and along with him Reinhold, whom the hoop had struck rather sharply, and who felt as if every limb was benumbed, strode back into the town in very low spirits. Then they heard a soft sighing and groaning behind a hedge. They stood still, and a tall figure at once rose up; they immediately recognised Conrad, and began to withdraw timidly. But he addressed them in a tearful voice, saying, "You need not be so frightened at me, my good comrades;

of course you take me for a devilish murderous brute, but I am not — indeed I am not so. I could not do otherwise; I ought to have struck down the fat old master, and by rights I ought to go along with you and do it now , if I only could. But no, no; it's all over. Remember me to pretty Rose, whom I love so above all reason. Tell her I will bear her flowers on my heart all my life long, I will adorn myself with them when I— but she will perhaps hear of me again some day. Farewell! farewell! my good, brave comrades." And Conrad ran away across the field without once stopping.

Reinhold said, "There is something peculiar about this young fellow; we can't weigh or measure this deed by any ordinary standard. Perhaps the future will unfold to us the secret that has lain heavy upon his breast."

1 The word "prince" is expressed in German by two distinct words; one, like the English word, designates a member of a royal or reigning house; the other is used as a simple title, often official, ranking above duke. The Bishop of Bamberg was in this latter sense a prince of the empire.

Reinhold leaves Master Martin's house.

If formerly there had been merry days in Master Martin's workshop, so now they were proportionately dull. Reinhold, incapable of work, remained confined to his room; Martin, his wounded arm in a sling, was incessantly abusing the good-for-nothing stranger-apprentice, and railing at him for the mischief he had wrought Rose, and even Dame Martha and her children, avoided the scene of the rash savage deed, and so Frederick's blows fell dull and melancholy enough, like a woodcutter's in a lonely wood in winter time, for to Frederick it was now left to finish the big cask alone, and a hard task it was.

And soon his mind and heart were possessed by a profound sadness, for he believed he had now clear proofs of what he had for a long time feared. He no longer had any doubt that Rose loved Reinhold. Not only had she formerly shown many a kindness to Reinhold alone, and to him alone given many a sweet word, but now — it was as plain as noonday — since Reinhold could no longer come to work. Rose too no longer thought of going out, but preferred to stay indoors, no doubt to wait upon and take good care of her lover. On Sundays, when all the rest set out gaily, and Master Martin, who had recovered to some extent of his wound, invited him to walk with him and Rose to the Allerwiese, he refused the invitation; but, burdened with trouble and the bitter pain of disappointed love, he hastened off alone to the village and the hill where he had first met with Reinhold. He threw himself down in the tall grass where the flowers grew, and as he thought how that the beautiful star of hope which had shone before him all along his homeward path had now suddenly set in the blackness of night after he had reached his goal, and as he thought how that this step which he had taken was like the vain efforts of a dreamer stretching out his yearning arms after an empty vision of air,— the tears fell from his eyes and dropped upon the flowers, which bent their little heads as if sorrowing for the young journeyman's great unhappiness. Without his being exactly conscious of it, the painful sighs which escaped his labouring breast assumed the form of words, of musical notes, and he sang this song:—

My star of hope,
Where hast thou gone?
Alas! thy glory rises up —
Thy glory sweet, far from me now —
And pours its light on others down.
Ye rustling evening breezes, rouse you,
Blow on my breast,
Awake all joy that kills,
Awake all pain that brings to death,
So that my sore and bleeding heart,
Steeped to the core in bitter tears,
May break in yearning comfortless.
Why whisper ye, ye darksome trees?
So softly and like friends together?
And why, O golden skirts of sky.

Look ye so kindly down on me?
Show me my grave;
For that is now my haven of hope,
Where I shall calmly, softly sleep.

And as it often happens that the very greatest trouble, if
only it can find vent in tears and words, softens down into a
gentle melancholy, mild and painless, and that often a faint
glimmer of hope appears then in the soul, so it was with
Frederick; when he had sung this song he felt wonderfully
strengthened and comforted The evening breezes and the
darksome trees that he had called upon in his song rustled and
whispered words of consolation; and like the sweet dreams of
distant glory or of distant happiness, golden streaks of light
worked their way up across the dusky sky. Frederick rose to
his feet, and went down the hill into the village. He almost
fancied that Reinhold was walking beside him as he did on
the day they first found each other; and all the words which
Reinhold had spoken again recurred to his mind. And as
his thoughts dwelt upon Reinhold's story about the contest
between the two painters who were friends, then the scales
fell from his eyes. There was no doubt about it; Reinhold
must have seen Rose before and loved her. It was only his
love for her which had brought him to Nuremberg to Master
Martin's, and by the contest between the two painters
he meant simply and solely their own — Reinhold's and
Frederick's — rival wooing of beautiful Rose. The words that
Reinhold had then spoken rang again in his ears,—"Honest

contention for the same prize, without any malicious reserve, ought to unite true friends and knit their hearts still closer together, instead of setting them at variance. There should never be any place in noble minds for petty envy or malicious hatred." "Yes," exclaimed Frederick aloud, "yes, friend of my heart, I will appeal to you without any reserve, you yourself shall tell me if all hope for me is lost."

It was approaching noon when Frederick tapped at Reinhold's door. As all remained still within, he pushed open the door, which was not locked as usual, and went in. But the moment he did so he stood rooted to the spot. Upon an easel, the glorious rays of the morning sun falling upon it, was a splendid picture, Rose in all the pride of her beauty and charms, and life size. The maul-stick lying on the table, and the wet colours of the palette, showed that some one had been at work on the picture quite recently. "O Rose, Rose!— By Heaven!" sighed Frederick. Reinhold, who had entered behind him unperceived, clapped him on the shoulder and asked, smiling, "Well, now, Frederick, what do you say to my picture!" Then Frederick pressed him to his heart and cried, "Oh you splendid fellow — you are indeed a noble artist. Yes, it's all clear to me now. You have won the prize — for which I— poor me!— had the hardihood to struggle. Oh! what am I in comparison with you? And what is my art against yours? And yet I too had some fine ideas in my head. Don't laugh at me, dear Reinhold; but, look you, I thought what a grand thing it would be to model Rose's lovely figure and cast it in the finest silver. But that's all childishness, whilst you

— you — Oh! how sweetly she smiles upon you, and how delightfully you have brought out all her beauty. O Reinhold! Reinhold! you happy, happy fellow! Ay, and it has all come about as you said long ago. We have both striven for the prize and you have won it: you could not help but win it, and I shall still continue to be your friend with all my heart But I must leave this house — my home: I cannot bear it, I should die if I were to see Rose again. Please forgive me, my dear, dear, noble friend. To-day, this very moment, I will go — go away into the wide world, where my trouble, my unbearable misery, is sending me." And thus speaking, Frederick was hastening out of the apartment, but Reinhold held him fast, saying gently, "You shall not go; for things may turn out quite different from what you think. It is now time for me to tell you all that I have hitherto kept silence about. That I am not a cooper but a painter you are now well aware, and I hope a glance at this picture will convince you that I am not to be ranked amongst the inferior artists. Whilst still young I went to Italy, the land of art; there I had the good fortune to be accepted as a pupil by renowned masters, who fostered into living fire the spark which glowed within me. Thus it came to pass that I rapidly rose into fame, that my pictures became celebrated throughout all Italy, and the powerful Duke of Florence1 summoned me to his court. At that time I would not hear a word about German art, and without having seen any of your pictures, I talked a good deal of nonsense about the coldness, the bad drawing, and the hardness of your Dürer and your Cranach.2 But one day a picture-dealer

brought a small picture of the Madonna by old Albrecht to
the Duke's gallery, and it made a powerful and wonderful
impression upon me, so that I turned away completely from
the voluptuousness of Italian art, and from that very hour
determined to go back to my native Germany and study there
the masterpieces upon which my heart was now set I came
to Nuremberg here, and when I beheld Rose I seemed to
see the Madonna who had so wonderfully stirred my heart,
walking in bodily form on earth. I had the same experiences
as you, dear Frederick; the bright flames of love flashed up
and consumed me, mind and heart and soul. I saw nothing, I
thought of nothing, but Rose; all else had vanished from my
mind; and even art itself only retained its hold upon me in so
far as it enabled me to draw and paint Rose again and again
— hundreds of times. I would have approached the maiden
in the free Italian way; but all my attempts proved fruitless.
There was no means of securing a footing of intimacy in
Master Martin's house in any insidious way. At last I made
up my mind to sue for Rose directly, when I learned that
Master Martin had determined to give his daughter only to
a good master-cooper. Straightway I formed the adventurous
resolve to go and learn the trade of cooperage in Strasburg,
and then to come and work in Master Martin's work-shop.
I left all the rest to the ordering of Providence. You know in
what way I carried out my resolve; but I must now also tell
you what Master Martin said to me some days ago. He said
I should make a skilful cooper and should be a right dear
and worthy son-inlaw, for he saw plainly that I was seeking

82

to gain Rose's favour, and that she liked me right well." "Can
it then indeed well be otherwise?" cried Frederick, painfully
agitated "Yes, yes, Rose will be yours ; how came I, unhappy
wretch that I am, ever to hope for such happiness?" "You are
forgetting, my brother," Reinhold went on to say; "you are
forgetting that Rose herself has not confirmed this, which
our cunning Master Martin no doubt is well aware of. True
it is that Rose has always shown herself kind and charming
towards me, but a loving heart betrays itself in other ways.
Promise me, brother, to remain quiet for three days longer,
and to go to your work in the shop as usual. I also could
now go to work again, but since I have been busy with, and
wrapt up in this picture, I feel an indescribable disgust at
that coarse rough work out yonder. And, what is more, I can
never lay hand upon mallet again, let come what will. On the
third day I will frankly tell you how matters stand between
me and Rose. If I should really be the lucky one to whom she
has given her love, then you may go your way and make trial
of the experience that time can cure the deepest wounds."
Frederick promised to await his fate.

On the third day Frederick's heart beat with fear and
anxious expectation; he had in the meantime carefully
avoided meeting Rose. Like one in a dream he crept about
the workshop, and his awkwardness gave Master Martin, no
doubt, just cause for his grumbling and scolding, which was
not by any means customary with him. Moreover, the master
seemed to have encountered something that completely
spoilt all his good spirits. He talked a great deal about base

tricks and ingratitude, without clearly expressing what he meant by it. When at length evening came, and Frederick was returning towards the town, he saw not far from the gate a horseman coming to meet him, whom he recognised to be Reinhold. As soon as the latter caught sight of Frederick he cried, "Ha! ha! I meet you just as I wanted." And leaping from his horse, he slung the rein over his arm, and grasped his friend's hand. "Let us walk along a space beside each other," he said. "Now I can tell you what luck I have had with my suit." Frederick observed that Reinhold wore the same clothes which he had worn when they first met each other, and that the horse bore a portmanteau. Reinhold looked pale and troubled. "Good luck to you, brother," he began somewhat wildly; "good luck to you. You can now go and hammer away lustily at your casks; I will yield the field to you. I have just said adieu to pretty Rose and worthy Master Martin." "What!" exclaimed Frederick, whilst an electric thrill, as it were, shot through all his limbs —"what! you are going away now that Master Martin is willing to take you for his son-inlaw, and Rose loves you?" Reinhold replied, "That was only a delusion, brother, which your jealousy has led you into. It has now come out that Rose would have had me simply to show her dutifulness and obedience, but there's not a spark of love glowing in her ice-cold heart. Ha! ha! I should have made a fine cooper — that I should. Week-days scraping hoops and planing staves, Sundays walking beside my honest wife to St. Catherine's or St. Sebald's, and in the evening to the Allerwiese, year after year"—— "Nay, mock not," said Frederick, interrupting Reinhold's loud laughter, "mock not at the excellent burgher's simple, harmless life. If Rose does not really love you, it is not her fault; you are so passionate, so wild." "You are right," said Reinhold; "It is only the silly way I have of making as much noise as a spoilt child when I conceive I have been hurt. You can easily imagine that I spoke to Rose of my love and of her father's good-will. Then the tears started from her eyes, and her hand trembled in mine. Turning her face away, she whispered, 'I must submit to my father's will'— that was enough for me. My peculiar resentment, dear Frederick, will now let you see into the depths of my heart; I must tell you that my striving to win Rose was a deception, imposed upon me by my wandering mind. After I had finished Rose's picture my heart grew calm; and often, strange enough, I fancied that Rose was now the picture, and that the picture was become the real Rose. I detested my former coarse, rude handiwork; and when I came so intimately into contact with the incidents of common life, getting one's 'mastership' and getting married, I felt as if I were going to be confined in a dungeon and chained to the stocks. How indeed can the divine being whom I carry in my heart ever be my wife? No, she shall for ever stand forth glorious in youth, grace, and beauty, in the pictures — the masterpieces — which my restless spirit shall create. Oh! how I long for such things! How came I ever to turn away from my divine art? O thou glorious land, thou home of Art, soon again will I revel amidst thy cool and balmy airs." The friends had reached the place where the road which Reinhold intended to take turned to the left. "Here we will part," cried Reinhold, pressing Frederick to his heart in a long warm embrace; then he threw himself upon horseback and galloped away. Frederick stood watching him without uttering a word, and then, agitated by the most unaccountable feelings, he slowly wended his way homewards.

1 At this time Francesco I. (of the illustrious house of Medici) was Grand Duke of Tuscany , his father Cosimo I. having exchanged the title of Duke of Florence for that of Grand Duke of Tuscany in 1569. Francesco did much for the encouragement of art and science. He founded the well-known Uffizi Gallery, and it was in his reign that the Accademia Della Crusca was instituted.

2 Lucas Cranach occupies along with his contemporary Albrecht Dürer the first place in the ranks of German painters. Born in Upper Franconia in 1472 (died 1553), he secured the favour of the Elector of Saxony, and manifested extraordinary activity in several branches of painting.

How Frederick was driven out of the workshop by Master Martin.

The next day Master Martin was working away at the great cask for the Bishop of Bamberg in moody silence, nor could Frederick, who now felt the full bitterness of parting from Reinhold, utter a word either, still less break out into song. At last Master Martin threw aside his mallet, and crossing his arms, said in a muffled voice, "Well, Reinhold's gone. He was a distinguished painter, and has only been making a fool of me with his pretence of being a cooper. Oh! that I had only had an inkling of it when he came into my house along with you and bore himself so smart and clever, wouldn't I just have shown him the door! Such an open honest face, and so much deceit and treachery in his mind! Well, he's gone, and now you will faithfully and honestly stick to me and my handiwork. Who knows whether you may not become something more to me still — when you have become a skilful master and Rose will have you — well, you understand me, and may try to win Rose's favour." Forthwith he took up his mallet and worked away lustily again. Frederick did not know how to account for it, but Master Martin's words rent his breast, and a strange feeling of anxiety arose in his mind, obscuring every glimmer of hope. After a long interval Rose made a first appearance again in the workshop, but was very reserved, and, as Frederick to his mortification could see, her eyes were red with weeping. She has been weeping for him, she does love him, thus he said within himself, and he was quite unable to raise his eyes to her whom he loved with such an unutterable love.

The mighty cask was finished, and now Master Martin began to be blithe and in good humour again as he regarded this very successful piece of work. "Yes, my son," said he, clapping Frederick on the shoulder, "yes, my son, I will keep my word: if you succeed in winning Rose's favour and build a good sound masterpiece, you shall be my son-inlaw. And then you can also join the noble guild of the Meistersinger , and so win you great honour."

Master Martin's business now increased so very greatly that he had to engage two other journeymen, clever workmen, but rude fellows, quite demoralised by their long wanderings. Coarse jests now echoed in the workshop instead of the many pleasant talks of former days, and in place of Frederick and Reinhold's agreeable singing were now heard low and obscene ditties. Rose shunned the workshop, so that Frederick saw her but seldom, and only for a few moments at a time. And then when he looked at her with melancholy longing and sighed, "Oh! if I might talk to you again, dear Rose, if you were only as friendly again as at the time when Reinhold was still with us!" she cast down her eyes in shy confusion and whispered "Have you something to tell me, dear Frederick?" And Frederick stood like a statue, unable to speak a word, and the golden opportunity was quickly past, like a flash of lightning that darts across the dark red glow of the evening, and is gone almost before it is observed.

Master Martin now insisted that Frederick should begin

his masterpiece. He had himself sought out the finest, purest oak wood, without the least vein or flaw, which had been over five years in his wood-store, and nobody was to help Frederick except old Valentine. Not only was Frederick put more and more out of taste with his work by the rough journeymen, but he felt a tightness in his throat as he thought that this masterpiece was to decide over his whole life long. The same peculiar feeling of anxiety which he had experienced when Master Martin was praising his faithful devotion to his handiwork now grew into a more and more distinct shape in a quite dreadful way. He now knew that he should fail miserably and disgracefully in his work; his mind, now once more completely taken up with his own art, was fundamentally averse to it. He could not forget Reinhold and Rose's picture. His own art now put on again her full glory in his eyes. Often as he was working, the crushing sense of the unmanliness of his conduct quite overpowered him, and, alleging that he was unwell, he ran off to St. Sebald's Church. There he spent hours in studying Peter Fischer's marvellous monument, and he would exclaim, as if ravished with delight, "Oh, good God! Is there anything on earth more glorious than to conceive and execute such a work?" And when he had to go back again to his staves and hoops, and remembered that in this way only was Rose to be won, he felt as if burning talons were rending his bleeding heart, and as if he must perish in the midst of his unspeakable agony. Reinhold often came to him in his dreams and brought him striking designs for artistic castings, into which Rose's form was worked in most ingenious ways, now as a flower, now as an angel, with little wings. But there was always something wanting; he discovered that it was Rose's heart which Reinhold had forgotten, and that he added to the design himself. Then he thought he saw all the flowers and leaves of the work move, singing and diffusing their sweet fragrances, and the precious metals showed him Rose's likeness in their glittering surface. Then he stretched out his arms longingly after his beloved, but the likeness vanished as if in dim mist, and Rose herself, pretty Rose, pressed him to her loving heart in an ecstasy of passionate love.

His condition with respect to the unfortunate cooperage grew worse and worse, and more and more unbearable, and he went to his old master Johannes Holzschuer to seek comfort and assistance. He allowed Frederick to begin in his shop a piece of work which he, Frederick, had thought out and for which he had for some time been saving up his earnings, so that he could procure the necessary gold and silver. Thus it happened that Frederick was scarcely ever at work in Martin's shop, and his deathly pale face gave credence to his pretext that he was suffering from a consuming illness. Months went past, and his masterpiece, his great two-tun cask, was not advanced any further. Master Martin was urgent upon him that he should at least do as much as his strength would allow, and Frederick really saw himself compelled to go to the hated cutting block again and take the adze in hand. Whilst he was working, Master Martin drew near and examined the staves at which he was working;

and he got quite red in the face and cried, "What do you call this? What work is this, Frederick? Has a journeyman been preparing these staves for his 'mastership,' or a stupid apprentice who only put his nose into the workshop three days ago? Pull yourself together, lad: what devil has entered into you that you are making a bungle of things like this? My good oak wood,— and this your masterpiece! Oh! you awkward, imprudent boy!" Overmastered by the torture and agony which raged within him, Frederick was unable to contain himself any longer; so, throwing the adze from him he said, "Master, it's all over; no, even though it cost me my life, though I perish in unutterable misery, I cannot work any longer — no, I cannot work any longer at this coarse trade. An irresistible power is drawing me back to my own glorious art. Your daughter Rose I love unspeakably, more than anybody else on earth can ever love her. It is only for her sake that I ever entered upon this hateful work. I have now lost her, I know, and shall soon die of grief for love of her; but I can't help it, I must go back to my own glorious art, to my excellent old master, Johannes Holzschuer, whom I so shamefully deserted." Master Martin's eyes blazed like flashing candles. Scarce able to speak for rage, he stammered, "What! you too! Deceit and treachery! Dupe me like this! coarse trade — cooperage! Out of my eyes, you disgraceful fellow; begone with you!" And therewith he laid hold of poor Frederick by the shoulders and threw him out of the shop, which the rude journeymen and apprentices greeted with mocking laughter. But old Valentine folded his hands, and gazing thoughtfully before him, said, "I've noticed, that I have, the good fellow had something higher in his mind than our casks." Dame Martha shed many tears, and her boys cried and screamed for Frederick, who had often played kindly with them and brought them several lots of sweets.

Conclusion.

However angry Master Martin might feel towards Reinhold and Frederick, he could not but admit to himself that along with them all joy and all pleasure had disappeared from the workshop. Every day he was annoyed and provoked by the new journeymen. He had to look after every little trifle, and it cost him no end of trouble and exertion to get even the smallest amount of work done to his mind. Quite tired out with the cares of the day, he often sighed, "O Reinhold! O Frederick! I wish you had not so shamefully deceived me, I wish you had been good coopers." Things at last got so bad that he often contemplated the idea of giving up business altogether.

As he was sitting at home one evening in one of these gloomy moods, Herr Jacobus Paumgartner and along with him Master Johannes Holzschuer came in quite unexpectedly. He saw at once that they were going to talk about Frederick; and in fact Herr Paumgartner very soon turned the conversation upon him, and Master Holzschuer at once began to say all he could in praise of the young fellow. It was his opinion that Frederick with his industry and his gifts would certainly not only make an excellent goldsmith, but also a most admirable art-caster, and would tread in Peter Fischer's footsteps. And now Herr Paumgartner began to reproach Master Martin in no gentle terms for his unkind treatment of his poor journeyman Frederick, and they both urged him to give Rose to the young fellow to wife when he was become a

93

skilful goldsmith and caster,— that is, of course, in case she looked with favour upon him,— for his affection for her tingled in every vein he had. Master Martin let them have their say out, then he doffed his cap and said, smiling, "That's right, my good sirs, I'm glad you stand up so bravely for the journeyman who so shamefully deceived me. That, however, I will forgive him; but don't ask that I should alter my fixed resolve for his sake; Rose can never be anything to him." At this moment Rose entered the room, pale and with eyes red with weeping, and she silently placed wine and glasses on the table. "Well then," began Herr Holzschuer, "I must let poor Frederick have his own way; he wants to leave home for ever. He has done a beautiful piece of work at my shop, which, if you, my good master, will allow, he will present to Rose as a keepsake; look at it." Whereupon Master Holzschuer produced a small artistically-chased silver cup, and handed it to Master Martin, who, a great lover of costly vessels and such like, took it and examined it on all sides with much satisfaction. And indeed a more splendid piece of silver work than this little cup could hardly be seen. Delicate chains of vine-leaves and roses were intertwined round about it, and pretty angels peeped up out of the roses and the bursting buds, whilst within, on the gilded bottom of the cup, were engraved angels lovingly caressing each other. And when the clear bright wine was poured into the cup, the little angels seemed to dance up and down as if playing prettily together. "It is indeed an elegant piece of work," said Master Martin, "and I will keep it if Frederick will take the double of what it is worth in good gold pieces." Thus speaking, he filled the cup and raised it to his lips. At this moment the door was softly opened, and Frederick stepped in, his countenance pale and stamped with the bitter, bitter pain of separating for ever from her he held dearest on earth. As soon as Rose saw him she uttered a loud piercing cry, "O my dearest Frederick!" and fell almost fainting on his breast. Master Martin set down the cup, and on seeing Rose in Frederick's arms opened his eyes wide as if he saw a ghost. Then he again took up the cup without speaking a word, and looked into it; but all at once he leapt from his seat and cried in a loud voice, "Rose, Rose, do you love Frederick?" "Oh!" whispered Rose, "I cannot any longer conceal it, I love him as I love my own life; my heart nearly broke when you sent him away." "Then embrace your betrothed, Frederick; yes, yes, your betrothed, Frederick," cried Master Martin. Paumgartner and Holzschuer looked at each other utterly bewildered with astonishment, but Master Martin, holding the cup in his hand, went on, "By the good God, has it not all come to pass as the old lady prophesied?—

'A vessel fair to see he'll bring,
In which the spicy liquid foams.
And bright, bright angels gaily sing.
... The vessel fair with golden grace,
Lo! him who brings it in the house,
Thou wilt reward with sweet embrace.
And, an thy lover be but true,
Thou need'st not wait thy father's kiss.'

95

"O Stupid fool I have been! Here is the vessel fair to see, the angels — the lover — Ay! ay! gentlemen; it's all right now, all right now; my son-inlaw is found."

Whoever has had his mind ever confused by a bad dream, so that he thought he was lying in the deep cold blackness of the grave, and suddenly he awakens in the midst of the bright spring-tide full of fragrance and sunshine and song, and she whom he holds dearest on earth has come to him and has cast her arms about him, and he can look up into the heaven of her lovely face,— whoever has at any time experienced this will understand Frederick's feelings, will comprehend his exceeding great happiness. Unable to speak a word, he held Rose tightly clasped in his arms as though he would never let her leave him, until she at length gently disengaged herself and led him to her father. Then he found his voice, "O my dear master, is it all really true? You will give me Rose to wife, and I may go back to my art?" "Yes, yes," said Master Martin, "you may in truth believe it; can I do any other since you have fulfilled my old grandmother's prophecy? You need not now of course go on with your masterpiece." Then Frederick, perfectly radiant with delight, smiled and said, "No, my dear master, if it be pleasing to you I will now gladly and in good spirits finish my big cask — my last piece of work in cooperage — and then I will go back to the melting-furnace." "Yes, my good brave son," replied Master Martin, his eyes sparkling with joy, "yes, finish your masterpiece, and then we'll have the wedding."

Frederick kept his word faithfully, and finished the two-tun cask; and all the masters declared that it would be no easy task to do a finer piece of work, whereat Master Martin was delighted down to the ground, and was moreover of opinion that Providence could not have found for him a more excellent son-inlaw.

At length the wedding day was come, Frederick's masterpiece stood in the entrance hall filled with rich wine, and crowned with garlands. The masters of the trade, with the syndic Jacobus Paumgartner at their head, put in an appearance along with their housewives, followed by the master goldsmiths. All was ready for the procession to begin its march to St. Sebald's Church, where the pair were to be married, when a sound of trumpets was heard in the street, and a neighing and stamping of horses before Martin's house. Master Martin hastened to the bay-window. It was Herr Heinrich von Spangenberg, in gay holiday attire, who had pulled up in front of the house; a few paces behind him, on a high-spirited horse, sat a young and splendid knight, his glittering sword at his side, and high-coloured feathers in his baretta, which was also adorned with flashing jewels. Beside the knight, Herr Martin perceived a wondrously beautiful lady, likewise splendidly dressed, seated on a jennet the colour of fresh-fallen snow. Pages and attendants in brilliant coats formed a circle round about them. The trumpet ceased, and old Herr von Spangenberg shouted up to him, "Aha! aha! Master Martin, I have not come either for your wine cellar or for your gold pieces, but only because it is Rose's wedding day. Will you let me in, good master?"

Master Martin remembered his own words very well, and was a little ashamed of himself; but he hurried down to receive the Junker. The old gentleman dismounted, and after greeting him, entered the house. Some of the pages sprang forward, and upon their arms the lady slipped down from her palfrey; the knight gave her his hand and followed the old gentleman. But when Master Martin looked at the young knight he recoiled three paces, struck his hands together, and cried, "Good God! Conrad!" "Yes, Master Martin," said the knight, smiling, "I am indeed your journeyman Conrad. Forgive me for the wound I inflicted on you. But you see, my good master, that I ought properly to have killed you; but things have now all turned out different." Greatly confused, Master Martin replied, that it was after all better that he had not been killed; of the little bit of a cut with the adze he had made no account. Now when Master Martin with his new guests entered the room where the bridal pair and the rest were assembled, they were all agreeably surprised at the beautiful lady, who was so exactly like the bride, even down to the minutest feature, that they might have been taken for twin-sisters. The knight approached the bride with courtly grace and said, "Grant, lovely Rose, that Conrad be present here on this auspicious day. You are not now angry with the wild thoughtless journeyman who was nigh bringing a great trouble upon you, are you?" But as the bridegroom and the bride and Master Martin were looking at each other in great wonder and embarrassment, old Herr von Spangenberg said, "Well, well, I see I must help you out of your dream. This is my son Conrad, and here is his good, true wife, named Rose, like the lovely bride. Call our conversation to mind, Master Martin. I had a very special reason for asking you whether you would refuse your Rose to my son. The young puppy was madly in love with her, and he induced me to lay aside all other considerations and make up my mind to come and woo her on his behalf. But when I told him in what an uncourteous way I had been dismissed, he in the most nonsensical way stole into your house in the guise of a cooper, intending to win her favour and then actually to run away with her. But — you cured him with that good sound blow across his back; my best thanks for it. And now he has found a lady of rank who most likely is, after all, the Rose who was properly in his heart from the beginning."

Meanwhile the lady had with graceful kindness greeted the bride, and hung a valuable pearl necklace round her neck as a wedding present. "See here, dear Rose," she then said, taking a very withered bunch of flowers out from amongst the fresh blooming ones which she wore at her bosom —"see here, dear Rose, these are the flowers that you once gave my Conrad as the prize of victory; he kept them faithfully until he saw me, then he was unfaithful to you and gave them to me; don't be angry with me for it." Rose, her cheeks crimson, cast down her eyes in shy confusion, saying, "Oh! noble lady, how can you say so? Could the Junker then ever really love a poor maiden like me? You alone were his love, and it was only because I am called Rose, and, as they say here, something like you, that he wooed me, all the while thinking it was you."

A second time the procession was about to set out, when a young man entered the room, dressed in the Italian style, all in black slashed velvet, with an elegant lace collar and rich golden chains of honour hanging from his neck. "O Reinhold, my Reinhold!" cried Frederick, throwing himself upon the young man's breast. The bride and Master Martin also cried out excitedly, "Reinhold, our brave Reinhold is come!" "Did I not tell you," said Reinhold, returning Frederick's embrace with warmth,—"did I not tell you, my dear, dear friend, that things might turn out gloriously for you? Let me celebrate your wedding day with you; I have come a long way on purpose to do so; and as a lasting memento hang up in your house the picture which I have painted for you and brought with me." And then he called down to his two servants, who brought in a large picture in a magnificent gold frame. It represented Master Martin in his workshop along with his journeymen Reinhold, Frederick, and Conrad working at the great cask, and lovely Rose was just entering the shop. Everybody was astonished at the truth and magnificent colouring of the piece as a work of art. "Ay," said Frederick, smiling, "that is, I suppose, your masterpiece as cooper; mine is below yonder in the entrance-hall; but I shall soon make another." "I know all," replied Reinhold, "and rate you lucky. Only stick fast to your art; it can put up with more domesticity and such-like than mine."

At the marriage feast Frederick sat between the two Roses, and opposite him Master Martin between Conrad and Reinhold. Then Herr Paumgartner filled Frederick's cup up to the brim with rich wine, and drank to the weal of Master Martin and his brave journeymen. The cup went round; and first it was drained by the noble Junker Heinrich von Spangenberg, and after him by all the worthy masters who sat at the table — to the weal of Master Martin and his brave journeymen.